SOME LIKE IT DEADLY

GOING ROYAL
BOOK THREE

HEATHER LONG

For everyone who fights the good fight, who refuses to sit on the sidelines and stands tall in defense of those in need. For the brave souls who show up, speak up, and keep believing, even when the world doesn't. And for that magical truth we often forget: sometimes, it only takes one person to believe in you to change everything. This is for you.

FOREWORD

Dear Reader,

Thank you for picking up *Some Like it Deadly*. If this is your first book you've picked up from me, welcome, happy to have you along for the ride! If you've read me for a while, you might be thinking this is a very familiar title, and you wouldn't be wrong. The first draft of this book dates back to 2012 or 2013. It was later contracted by Carina Press, a digital imprint of Harlequin as the third in the Going Royal series and released in 2014.

This series does what I have loved so much about other romance series I read while growing up, taking a supporting character from an another book in the series and putting them front and center. In this case, we're taking *two* characters we've met previously and pairing them up. It's romantic suspense, undercover bodyguard, office romance, with a dash of royal connections and fake identities.

As I was working my way back through this

one, I had forgotten just how much I loved Richard and Kate. Kate is a badass who doesn't spend a lot of time saying she's a badass. She's professional, skilled, and very human. Richard is an overachiever, a guy damaged by a past and seems to be trying to make up for it constantly. He's also stubborn as hell, something he has in common with his best friend Armand and with Kate.

Needless to say, it sets the stage for some personality collisions as Kate does her best to protect the man who doesn't want a bodyguard, without letting him know she is there to be his bodyguard.

As with the first two, there's a great deal of rom com in this, but it also has the suspense and danger elements that my latest readers will know i enjoy so much.

Re-reading and working through this took me back to when I wrote it the first time. I've finally gotten the time and the distance to be able to look at it with clean eyes and refreshed enjoyment.

I know I always say I am so excited to share this with you, but I truly am delighted to take you on a journey with Richard and Kate.

Happy reading!

xoxo

Heather

CHAPTER I
KATE

The sharp trill of the phone split the silent darkness in half. Kate Braddock jerked upright and had the phone in her hand, and answered before her mind fully processed the steps from sleep to waking. Adrenaline flooded her system, but training kept her voice calm. "Braddock."

Too many middle-of-the-night phone calls heralded bad news.

"Kate." Peterson's voice sent relief chasing through the adrenaline pumping through her system. "My apologies for the odd hour." The head of security for Armand Dagmar personally and the Andraste Royal Family in general didn't sound remotely apologetic. Nor did he sound deeply concerned, which hopefully meant, Anna, her protectee and the fiancée of the grand duke was also fine.

Of course, as her boss, Peterson never sounded disturbed.

"It's fine, sir." She gave the perfunctory an-

1

swer and shoved a hand through her hair. The sharp tug helped fuel her sleepy mind. Slanting a look at the clock, she sighed. It was only four-thirty in the morning. On her day off—the single day she'd had off in weeks. "What can I do for you?"

"We have a delicate situation and I am going to be blunt, Braddock. You're actually the only woman for the job." Plunging right in and ripping off the Band-Aid was far preferable to beating around the bush. At this early hour, all she required were the specifics with no sugar coating involved.

"What's the job?" Pushing back the blankets, Kate rose and padded to the kitchen. She'd already set up the coffee maker the night before. All she had to do was hit the on switch.

"Richard Prentiss slipped his security detail this weekend." Prentiss was the grand duke's best friend, and he'd been involved in a rather spectacular car accident a few months earlier.

Kate was impressed—with Prentiss, not his security detail. How they let a wounded man slip them didn't bode well for their future in the business.

"He was beyond our supervision and out of communication range for nearly seven hours." And then as if anticipating her question, Peterson added. "He left his cell phone at the house, and returned via taxi looking none the worse for wear, but..."

"But he slipped his security." The loss had likely pinched the pride of a man as thorough as

Peterson. He was damn good at his job. She didn't envy the members of the detail who'd failed to keep the attorney under surveillance and safe. They wouldn't have their jobs much longer—if they hadn't been fired already. "So what does that have to do with me?"

"Mr. Prentiss informed the grand duke he would be returning to his regular duties at his office tomorrow and he wants the security detail pulled." In a reverse of his earlier bluntness, Peterson circled around to his point. Kate turned at the sound of the coffee maker finishing its job, and poured herself a mug of the dark blend. The process kept her busy and her mouth shut.

She was a good soldier, and well-trained. Peterson would get to what he wanted soon enough.

"Look, Braddock, the grand duke wants to appease Mr. Prentiss, but he's not prepared to remove security from him. Chatter has slowed, but it hasn't quieted fully. When we inserted you with Miss Novak, you downplayed your presence as personal security by acting as her assistant."

And there it was.

"You want me to do the same for Mr. Prentiss?" She hadn't been especially fond of deceiving Anna, but then she'd never had to lie to her directly either. Peterson and the grand duke had simply told her that Kate had been vetted by security and could act as her assistant. That Kate could do the job. The deception kept her in Anna's orbit. Every time Anna left the tower to work, Kate had gone with her.

"Yes, we've arranged to have his legal assistant head out on a worldwide cruise, all expenses paid. She leaves today, in about three and a half hours, I need you to meet with her and get everything you'll need to know about how to do the job because you'll be interviewing with him tomorrow. I'll have the car picking her up swing by to get you in ninety minutes." Peterson had thought of everything, his smug tone might be well deserved. Mr. Prentiss wasn't the easiest protectee.

So much for her day off. "Do you think that Mr. Prentiss is just going to hire me because his assistant left? I'm assuming he has others in that law firm he could borrow—"

"He could, obviously, but he and the grand duke are scheduled to have lunch later today and..." Peterson trailed off and actually sighed. "Let's just say that he'll receive the news of his assistant's departure under controlled circumstances and the grand duke will then volunteer your services. We'll get you in the door, but you'll need to secure the position."

How very Machiavellian of the grand duke.

"You're asking me to protect someone who doesn't want a detail and who won't know what I'm doing." The potential for clusterfuck was enormous. Anna had been a similar case, but she'd also had a full detail on her at all times in addition to Kate. "What kind of detail is Prentiss going to have?"

"A discreet one." He paused a beat, then continued, "Kate, I know this isn't the easiest assignment. I wouldn't ask you to do it if I didn't think you were fully capable of it. The grand duke is worried about Mr. Prentiss's visibility. We can't properly secure him without his cooperation. You will have backup, but they could be twenty seconds out."

And twenty seconds could be the difference between life and death.

"Understood." She drained her coffee and glanced at the wall clock. "I'll be ready in ninety minutes for the car."

Once he had her agreement, Peterson disconnected the call and Kate carried her cell phone into the second bedroom that she'd converted into a workout room. Five minutes later, she was running on the treadmill. Too wired to go back to sleep, she checked the time.

It was nearly noon in Germany, her brother usually had Sundays off and spent them watching recorded sports. After hitting her brother's contact, she waited. When he answered on the second ring, the last knot of tension Peterson's middle of the night call had wound in her soul relaxed. "Hey, Beany Baby, how are you?"

His groan made her laugh.

He was okay. Alive.

She could handle everything else.

RICHARD

"I'm not going to lie to you, Ms. Braddock—the job won't be easy. This position demands travel at least forty percent of the time. Where I go, you go. When I need a file, I need you to pull it up. You have to anticipate last minute changes and I may be calling or texting you at three in the morning to come in because we need to have a brief in front of a judge at eight." Richard Prentiss leaned back in his chair and studied the blonde woman seated across from him. Her calm, cool eyes—he couldn't tell if they were hazel or just a very pale brown—betrayed no hint of concern. Considering he was offering her well-compensated indentured servitude, he'd hoped for a little more bite in her responses. "This is a steep learning curve and I wish that Miranda had given me more notice before she left, but we have to work with what we have." He wasn't sure what frustrated him more—Miranda leaving on such short notice or that she left at all. Miranda Keen had worked for him since he'd hung his shingle and despite Armand's copious attempts to fund his law firm, Richard had built his client list from the ground up. No one knew him better than Miranda—and no one deserved to come into a windfall as much as she, either. He'd paid her well, but that didn't mean she wanted to spend the rest of her life working sixteen-hour days.

"That won't be a problem, Mr. Prentiss. I'm used to a tough schedule and travel." Of course she was. Kate Braddock had been recommended to him by Armand during their racquetball game —the first he'd been able to play since a car accident laid him up some months before. Losing a kidney and his spleen meant a lot of changes in his routine, but he was finally well enough to kick his armed babysitters to the curb. He'd understood the need for increased security, particularly during his recovery, but he didn't like having a posse of heavily armed babysitters entrenching themselves in his life, tearing it apart, and dictating his movements. Armand hadn't liked the idea, but as Richard had informed his best friend, he could stuff it.

"True, you've been with Anna the last few months." Richard grimaced and drummed his fingers against the resume sitting atop her personnel file. The speed of Miranda's departure meant he had to cut corners to find her replacement. Kate's previous stint with Anna meant he didn't have to worry about a background check. She'd have been vetted by at least two different security agencies. "How will she handle your departure?"

"I believe the recommendation came from Miss Novak, Mr. Prentiss. She has a full staff to help with her foundation responsibilities and an additional two secretaries beyond myself. Her precise words were that she would miss me personally, but professionally she was covered." The wry response suggested a sense of humor and Richard nodded, but continued to drum his fingers. It was all a little too neat for his level of comfort. The world did not provide easy solutions—and in his experience, if one didn't examine every angle of a potential Trojan horse, one deserved to be burned.

And she comes recommended by Armand who wants me safe, so chances are she's exactly what she appears to be.

Still.

"The better question, I believe, is will we work well together?" She eyed him coolly as she flipped the questions to him. "Do you have any particularly annoying habits that I might object to? Are you a vegetarian perhaps? Or someone who speaks with their mouth full of food? Do you eat while you dictate your notes? Do you prefer MP3s or in person dictation? What types of confidentiality contracts am I expected to sign? Will I receive any type of additional compensation for the level of disruption in my life? When you have romantic liaisons will you expect me to wait in the other room on the off chance of a three-a.m. emergency?"

The rapid-fire questions eliminated his initial assessment. He grinned, she definitely had bite. "I have no idea if we'll work well together, but my initial impression is yes. I have no annoying habits that I'm aware of, though I've been told I'm an ass on more than one occasion." He let that hang out there to see what she would do with it.

"You're an attorney, Mr. Prentiss. I would expect you received your certification in being an ass about the same time you passed the bar." Sharp, dry and to the point.

She answered every question, and had retaliated with a few of her own.

He liked her.

"I never talk when my mouth is full." He layered innuendo along the words on purpose. Anna and Armand's recommendation aside, he needed a personal assistant who could do her job in the office and not on her back. Instead of rising to the bait, she merely lifted her eyebrows and waited. Impressed, he continued. "Let's see, there is a very good chance that I will dictate notes while consuming a meal, but I expect you'll be eating at the same time, so we'll adjust accordingly. I tend to record notes on my cell phone when I drive and I'll text you the voice memos as needed."

Shifting her personnel folder to the side, he held out a fifteen-page contract and sobered. All personal quirks aside, he needed some assurances. "This is the confidentiality agreement. It's ironclad and it stipulates on all terms that it remains enforced whether you work for me for five seconds, five months or five decades. What we discuss, what information passes in my office, is between you and I and absolutely no one else. I don't care if the police are questioning you or the President of the United States—privileged defines every communication. If you can't handle that, we stop right here."

"Unless you're planning to assassinate the president or in some way create mass havoc such as harboring a terrorist, I have no problems with signing that contract." Utterly unruffled, she didn't pause to consider her response. "I will, of course, insist that you add to those caveats. Privileged information does not allow you to compromise my integrity or make me complicit in a crime." The blunt force of personality added another tick into the pro column.

He extended the sheaf of papers. "Section four, paragraph three, subsection A—it's a personal morality clause. It stipulates if you believe a crime is being planned or has been committed that has caused, will cause, or may cause duress or undue distress to you or another living being, you may waive the privilege—in only that issue —to report it."

"I'm not sure whether to be disturbed or impressed that you have that in a confidentiality agreement." She took the papers and flipped to the section he'd indicated, a tiny line forming between her brows. "The fact that you've already considered it enough to put it in the contract suggests you've been burned."

Smiling at the implied question, he spread his hands. "I'm afraid that's confidential. However, read through and make sure you understand it. Perhaps consult an attorney and if you can do that in the next—" he checked his watch, "—fifteen minutes, that would be great. I have a backlog of cases and briefs that need my attention."

Most people would have snapped to their feet at the urgency, but she didn't. Instead she rested the contract in her lap and stared at him. At his raised eyebrows, a smile turned up the corners of her mouth. "You failed to answer the final two questions."

Smart. Detail-oriented. Capable of challenging him. Security clearance vetted by the royal family. If she was half as good at doing her job as she was the interview, he might survive Miranda abandoning him. Picking up an envelope, he passed it over. It contained a check he'd had drawn on his way to the meeting. "That contains your stipend for this month. The stipend is a living fund and completely separate from your paycheck which, as previously discussed, is considerable. You will have access to a corporate credit card. I'll order it today, but I expect it within the week. You may use the card to charge anything you need while working or on the job—hotel rooms, meals, clothing—provided you document the expenses."

She didn't open the envelope. Professional—but she would have had to be. He knew her work with Anna, particularly in recent months, meant access to discretionary funding, which added another facet to her worth in the position. Richard made a mental note to call Anna later and make sure she could part with Kate Braddock—that seemed fair.

"And as for my 'liaisons.'" No, he hadn't forgotten that question. "I keep a strictly personal-professional line in all areas."

"Excellent. Do you have any other questions for me?"

He hadn't, but then changed his mind. "Do *you* have any annoying habits that will interfere with our ability to work together? Do you eat with your mouth open? Prefer meals laden with onions or garlic? Can't function without coffee? A boyfriend or significant other that might object to my three-a.m. calls? The last thing I need is a riled lover accusing me of trying to seduce you." It was really none of his damn business, but she'd started it.

"No, sir. I'm practically perfect in every way." She rose, expression absolutely serene. "And I have no interest in Wyoming for a ranch, but Montana, I hear, is very nice. You have twelve minutes before your call. If you'll excuse me, I'll review this contract."

He opened his mouth to ask her what she meant and then snapped it shut again.

A few months before, when he'd been in the hospital, Armand had tossed an accusation his way in a fit of pique.

Armand had laughed. "You make fun now, but sooner or later you're going to meet a woman who ties you up in knots. And we'll see who is cracking jokes then."

"Not gonna happen. I'll find me some nice secretary who thinks the boss is her meal ticket, she'll be all yes sir and no sir and thank you very much sir and we'll have four kids and a dog and a summer ranch in Wyoming." Richard had snorted. "Now, get the hell out of here and find your girl, or sources close to the prince are going to report you knocked her up."

Armand was a dead man. "Of course." He mentally applauded his steady voice, but respect shifted through him as he watched her leave his office. The room's orderly appearance was a testament to Miranda's handling of everything during his recovery—thank God she hadn't left him then. Checking his watch after the door closed behind Kate, he picked up the phone and dialed the prince's private line. Armand answered on the second ring.

"I take it Miss Braddock made it to her appointment on time?" Laughter danced behind the European accent.

"You're a dick," Richard said by way of answer. "And she's perfect. So go ahead and chortle."

Armand laughed. "Good. I have another call and Gretchen is giving me the eye. Time for another game tomorrow?"

"Sorry, Your Highness, some of us have to work for a living. How's," he paused and flipped open his tablet to look at his calendar. "Friday?"

"I'll have to rearrange some items."

"You're the one who wants to play." Richard appreciated the sentiment. "I have another call to make too. Give Anna my regards."

"Right. Rick?" Worry coated his tone.

"Yeah?" Richard waited, Armand hadn't been thrilled with his decision to go back to work and while he might be Richard's most loyal client and oldest friend—he wasn't the only one.

"Never mind." The prince sighed, apparently ceding the argument without making it. "Don't overdo it." The last came out a direct order, but one made out of concern rather than arrogance. The call ended as abruptly as they'd begun it, but after more than a decade of friendship it didn't bother him. Picking up Kate's personnel file, he slid it into the bottom right drawer and locked it. He would read through the rest of it later. He checked his watch again. Another seven minutes until the conference call with the judge.

Fortunately, from the way Miranda organized his calendar, he accessed the file he needed on the tablet by choosing the date and the meeting. Reacquainting himself with the case took him four minutes more.

At two minutes until his phone was due to ring, Kate returned and set the contract down in front of him. She flipped to the next to last page and had circled one sub-section. "We need to amend this to say both parties and I will sign it."

Curious, he reviewed the line.

This Agreement states the entire agreement between the parties concerning the disclosure of Confidential Information and supersedes any prior agreements, understandings, or representations with respect thereto.

Changing "the" to "both" would include him in the confidentiality clause of any information she might share with him. With sixty seconds on the clock, he crossed out the word, wrote in "both" and initialed it, before passing over the pen. She turned the sheets around and leaned over the desk. A hint of vanilla and hazelnut tickled his nostrils and he eyed the way she added her initials to each page and then signed the last one before passing him the pen back.

He added his signature and the phone rang.

Claiming the handset, Kate straightened. "Richard Prentiss's office, this is Kate. How may I help you?"

~

THE AFTERNOON FLEW by in a flurry of phone calls and Richard had to give Kate a hell of a lot of credit. She'd parachuted into the chaos and rode out the storm with an easy smile and cool demeanor. He was on his fifth call of the day, and weary as hell. Judge Ryan's intractable position was sending his blood pressure skyrocketing, when she stood and set her digital tablet, steno pad, and pen on the desk, inviting his attention.

"Forgive me, Mr. Prentiss," Kate had interjected in the midst of the judge's tirade about the number of delays the case had experienced—none of which had anything to do with Richard's recent stint in the hospital and subsequent recovery.

"Miss Braddock?" Richard stared at her. Interrupting a judge was never a good idea, but she didn't wait for the man on the speakerphone to voice his objections.

"You have another call with Judge Wilkerson in five minutes and you need to take your medication." She walked to the wet bar on the far side of his office, opened the fridge and retrieved a can of soda, a sandwich container, then nudged the fridge shut with her leg before retrieving a small prescription bottle from the shelf above.

"If you have Wilkerson in five, Prentiss, you

should take your medication before the call."
Judge Ryan gruffed, his contrary tone less biting.
"You have a continuance for one week. I expect
the brief on my desk no later than Monday
morning at nine or I will rule in favor of the
plaintiff. Am I clear?"

Surprised, but unwilling to look the gift horse
in the mouth, Richard straightened. "Yes, sir.
Thank you, Judge Ryan." The call clicked off and
Kate set the clear plastic container holding a deli
sandwich down in front of him, along with the
can of regular Coke and the prescription bottle.
Without missing a beat, she picked up her steno
and added a notation regarding the brief, the case
number, the time and date it was due.

"I don't have a call with Wilkerson. How did
you know I needed these?" Richard asked, but he
opened the prescription bottle because she was
right.

He *was* due for his medication.

Losing his spleen meant he had to take sup-
plements regularly. Losing his kidney meant
watching his liquid intake, hence the one can of
soda he permitted himself per day, but how the
hell had Kate known? They hadn't had a chance
to go over any of those details.

"Ms. Keen kept meticulous notes and set up
several reminders in her calendar." Kate turned
the digital pad around and pointed to the message that had popped up. *Remind Richard to take
medication. Must be taken with food.*

"Oh." Mollified, he popped the can open, and
tossed back his two pills. "And Judge Wilkerson?"

"According to the notes taped to the bottom of her keyboard, there are five judges' calls never to be missed or ignored. Wilkerson sits at the top of the list and is labeled as a total PIA." Kate's voice betrayed no hint of humor, despite the gleam in her eyes. "I hazarded a guess that if the judges' names warranted that type of documentation, they might give Judge Ryan room to walk back his temper."

So she'd noticed the judge's testy tone growing more recalcitrant through the call. "I don't think I paid Miranda enough," Richard mused then took a bite of the sandwich. "When you have a chance, pull Leonard v Johnson file. I want to go over the previous two continuances. They were from the plaintiff. This is the first time I've asked for one. But I have to wonder what pressure the judge is getting." The judge had been more amenable on the first case he'd called about—one that had begun as a simple divorce—but the plaintiff was a highly respected plastic surgeon and he and his attorney had gone after the soon-to-be ex-wife with everything they had. The sheer malice in their initial filing had incited Richard's protective instincts and he'd usurped the case from one of his associates. "And put a call into Mrs. Ramsey, let's see if she has time to sit down with me this week."

Kate nodded and added another note to the steno. "You have another phone call in thirty minutes. Do you want me to hold your calls so you can take a break?"

Did he look tired? Rubbing the back of his

neck, he shook his head. "I'd rather get a few letters done. I'm supposed to be at a charity function at six-thirty—oh, that reminds me. Do you have evening wear?"

"Cocktail or formal?" She'd set the steno down then worked on her tablet.

"Both, but for tonight—cocktail." The event was a minor one, but he hadn't been able to do much for it over the intervening months and he wanted to put in an appearance. "We can go, mingle for about an hour and then get dinner and go over the rest of the week." He'd devoured most of the sandwich, a hell of a lot hungrier than he'd realized. Of course, he'd skipped lunch to interview Kate then been on the phone since.

"Very well. I'll send someone to pick up a dress for me." She flipped the tablet around and passed it over to him. The case file for Leonard versus Johnson was open. Sliding his finger over the screen, he paged through. Kate retrieved the empty container and the prescription bottle, disposing of the first and returning the latter to the shelf.

"We can swing by on the way to it, if you think you can change fast." It would save time. "And I can dictate a few letters in the car." Richard grimaced and dragged his attention up from the file. "I'm sorry, Miss Braddock, you really are going to have to jump in the deep end this week. While I do demand a lot, it won't always be this chaotic."

"It's not a problem. I'll adjust and make sure I keep an array of clothing choices on hand for future events. I noticed you have the scholarship charity dinner on Thursday, but you RSVP'd as a maybe. Should I decline or accept it?"

"Accept. It was only a maybe to get Armand off my ass." When his friend had been trying to manipulate him into declining any number of events so he'd stay home. "That will be full formal and I have a half-dozen clients who will also be attending in addition to the grand duke, so we're not going to have a lot of time to enjoy the function. Do you need something to eat? I have more sandwiches stocked." It was the one habit Miranda drilled into him. She had a service stock the fridge weekly and he had to eat at least half of them or she'd start canceling his appointments. *I wonder if Miranda put that in her notes? Would Kate make the same kinds of threats?*

"I'm fine, thank you. Water?" She'd retrieved two bottles and returned to the desk before he could nod. A line in the second continuance held his attention and he had to read it three times.

Leonard stipulated he'd suffered grievous injuries during an armed robbery in Johnson's convenience store. The owner, Johnson, had also been injured—he'd sustained a gunshot wound to his shoulder. Total physical damages amounted to about fifteen thousand dollars, but loss of work and having to close his store for repairs while in the hospital had cost Johnson considerably more. Leonard's suit cited Johnson's refusal to cooperate with the armed robbers—identified as two men of Latin descent in their late teens, early twenties. Though they were suspected in a string of related crimes, neither subject had been apprehended.

When Leonard brought suit against Johnson, he maintained he'd been unable to work, had suffered mentally, physically, and emotionally following the attack and had a doctor diagnose him with PTSD. But the second continuance had been asked for and sustained because Leonard had to be out of town.

The judge had granted the request because Richard had been in the hospital and still recovering. Richard hadn't thought much of it, but he'd also been on painkillers. Scrolling through the pages, he looked for the attending evidence attached to the continuance—where had Leonard needed to be that he couldn't be in court?

Reaching for the phone, he punched in the number for one of the investigators he kept on retainer. "Hey, Mitch, it's Richard."

"Welcome back, man. How's your first day?" A former member of the LAPD, Mitch Blake had taken medical disability after a drunk driver left him with a permanent limp and partial hearing loss, but neither injury had done anything to damage his sharp mind.

They'd met via a case when Richard had defended another officer in a civil suit. Mitch had been honest about his fellow officer's anger management issues, but adamant that he'd been in a solid frame of mind during the arrest. After his accident, Richard had offered his services free of charge and they'd worked together on several cases since. Mitch was a straight shooter, and he'd helped Richard with other delicate cases including two relocations.

He trusted him.

"Busy as hell. Look, I know you've probably got a lot on your plate and this may be nothing, but I need a fast turnaround on some information." Richard picked up a pen and twirled it around between two fingers. Across from him, Kate held up her notepad with a single question mark on it.

"Whatcha got?" Brisk and to the point—it was why he and Mitch worked so well together.

Shaking his head in answer to her silent query, he tapped his pen on the desk. "John Leonard, age 42. Lives at 4421 Wilkins Avenue—he stipulated that on April 14th he had to be out of town and was unable to attend court. Can you find out where he went?"

"Sure thing, boss. Anything else?"

"No, that's all for now—anything you can pull together on that and if it smells fishy...?"

"Don't worry, I'll drop a line. Talk to ya soon." Mitch hung up and Richard drummed his pen again. He'd missed something when he'd reviewed those papers and being medicated didn't excuse it.

Not when Brett Johnson had hung his future on Richard defending him. If he lost, Johnson would lose his store, his life's work, and his retirement. The man didn't deserve that.

One benefit of his own firm was the ability to take on any case he chose—like Johnson. His younger associates did a fair share of pro bono work, it was a requirement of their hiring into Prentiss and Associates, but some cases were personal for Richard and he kept them on the down low. Those details didn't leave his office.

Kate had taken it upon herself to remove his can of Coke and he hadn't finished it yet. Irritated, but forcing patience, he twisted the cap off the water bottle. After swallowing a long drink of water he nodded to her steno. She picked up her pen and looked at him expectantly. "Let's draft a letter to Mr. Johnson and alert him to the continuance, dated today. Brett, please accept my apologies for the many delays your case has faced over the last few months. I spoke to and obtained a continuance in the discovery phase today due to just returning to the office from my recovery. I also have some questions regarding the previous continuance. All briefs will be filed with Judge Ryan's office next Monday—add the date—and I will contact you when a trial date has been set. I know your concerns and I will do everything I can to resolve this matter prior to going to trial. I look forward to talking to you soon, sincerely—fill in the data."

He took another drink and watched her flip the page to begin the next letter. They'd managed six before his next call. Since he could handle talking to Armand's cousin Francesca about the upcoming release of her trust fund without Kate, he sent her out to take care of those letters.

Closing his eyes, Richard pinched the bridge of his nose. Alone, he could admit to the weariness dragging on him. He shouldn't have tried to play so hard on the court. He didn't have anything to prove with Armand—except he did. His best friend still blamed himself for the car accident and had all but buried Richard in bodyguards for the three months of his convalescence. Though Richard had read the reports from Armand's security team, as well as the investigation opened by the police department, he remembered very little of the actual accident.

That bothered him. He thrived on details, but the vague shadow of crunching metal and falling were all he'd been able to piece together. The doctors had told him he may never remember it.

Though his case remained open, everyone—Armand included—believed the accident was tied to the same group that tried to kill Armand. Richard was the face of the family, and it didn't matter that they had no conclusive proof, his best friend wouldn't let it go. Richard's injuries had scared Armand and he'd reacted accordingly.

Hell, he probably bribed that doctor to keep me on limited mobility.

Playing hard had been the only way to prove he was back up to snuff. Except—his side ached and he wanted that nap Kate had suggested earlier. Scrubbing a hand over his face, he hit the button for Kate's desk. "I won't typically ask for this, but I have to get on the phone with Francesca Grace to go over some inheritance issues. Do you mind heading down to the coffee kart in the lobby and picking me up a latte? Treat yourself to one too."

"Not a problem, Mr. Prentiss. Are you sure you don't want me to cancel the five o'clock call? You could have thirty minutes before we head to the function."

No, he wasn't sure. But he couldn't afford to show weakness to anyone. "The coffee will be fine, thank you."

He'd barely hung up and started to dial out again when the crash of a door slamming against the wall echoed from the outer office, followed by a very loud, very irate male voice.

CHAPTER 2
KATE

Heated voices in the hall alerted her to a problem. She was already on her feet when the door to her office burst open to reveal a red-faced man with a vein all but popping in his forehead. In the split-second between the door slamming and his mouth opening, she identified the intruder as Caucasian. Blood shot eyes. At least six feet. Brown hair not just receded, but in full retreat. And a distinctly off-kilter balance. He had no weapons in his hands, no telltale bulges under his jacket sleeves.

"Where the hell is he?" He demanded, stalking toward the door to Richard's office, but Kate stepped into his path, her right hand stiff and ready to jab.

"Mr. Prentiss is otherwise occupied." She kept her tone cordial and locked gazes with the infuriated man. His scowl seemed designed to intimidate. Unfortunately for him, Kate was far from impressed. "If you'd like to make an appointment, we can consult the calendar."

"Missy, get out of my way before I move you." The man's bellow offered another clue—it reeked of alcohol.

"That would be an assault charge." She had a panic button that would alert Prentiss's security detail, but she left it alone. Despite his antagonistic demeanor and threats, he'd stopped a good foot away from her. "One more step and we can make it battery. Now I'm sure whatever issue you have for Mr. Prentiss can be easily resolved. Why don't you take a seat?"

Most bullies got their jollies by inciting a reaction. By denying him one she hoped to defuse the situation. The door behind her opened and every muscle in Kate's body coiled. She didn't shift, keeping her full attention on the stranger.

"Dad." Richard's aggrieved tone eased the tension in her spine, but not her vigilance. "Are you seriously threatening my assistant?"

"Where's Miranda?" Richard's father looked past her to his son. Despite the filial acknowledgement, Kate didn't see any resemblance between the brute in front of her and the lean, dangerously handsome man she'd been working across from all day.

"She's not here, obviously. Ms. Braddock, please accept my apologies on behalf of my father. He's not usually quite so much of a jackass on first acquaintance." The tiredness simmering beneath his voice kept her on alert. "Dad, I have a call that I am now late for can this wait?"

"No, dammit." The man lurched forward, apparently intending to bulldoze right through

Kate. She made a split-second judgment call and blocked him by putting her foot right between his as he stepped. A calculated move—it was designed to look like she had attempted to get out of his way—and they collided. His already unsteady balance had him pitching to the side. She caught his arm and applied pressure as her knee glanced off the back of his.

She had to hit the desk with her hip, but he was seated in a chair and Richard had rushed forward to steady her. "My goodness, Mr. Prentiss— please accept my apologies for being in your way." Not that she felt an ounce of sorrow, but her cover had to be maintained.

"Are you alright?" Richard focused his concern on her and kept his hand on her elbow. At her nod he turned on his father. The transformation from exhausted to sharp attorney added a distinct edge to his expression. But instead of saying anything to the man, he reached over her desk and picked up the phone and dialed a three-digit code.

Security.

"This is Richard Prentiss. Benedict Prentiss is in Ms. Braddock's office, please send a couple of men up to escort him from the building and have a car deliver him home—do *not* let him drive." He hung up then folded his arms. "Ms. Braddock, if you don't mind waiting in my office."

"You have a call, Mr. Prentiss, and a very busy evening schedule. If you'd like to take care of it, I will see that this issue is handled." She kept her body angled between the two men. Whatever discord existed between them, his father was drunk and Richard could not afford additional injuries—especially not when he'd pushed himself so damn hard already.

A muscle flexed in Richard's jaw. "This is not covered in our employment contract. No one should have to put up with him." And didn't that speak volumes for the contentious relationship between the two.

"That's hardly a way to talk about your father when I'm sitting right here." Benedict Prentiss tried to stand, but sat back down abruptly. The bilious look on his face suggested the only real danger he posed now was to the carpeting.

"Mr. Prentiss, go make your call." Kate decided on a gentle coaxing tone. "We're on the clock and, as you can see, he's quite settled in the chair."

"You don't have to do this," Richard murmured, not quite turning his head and yet she could still feel the weight of his regard.

Yes, she did. "But you do need to make that call, and security is already on their way up." And would be fired if she were in charge.

He hesitated, seemingly aggravated on multiple levels and she didn't care for the way his jaw continued to tick. "I'll leave the door open. You stand in it so I can see you, if he gets stupid, just step all the way in and shut the door."

"So that's it?" Benedict struggled to his feet. "You just leave me with the skirt and go back to your high and mighty life?"

"Mr. Prentiss, you should sit before you fall

down." Kate moved to intercept the man and put a hand on his arm. This time she applied more than a little pressure and he sat immediately. "I'll get you some water and your car will be along directly."

Richard stood in the doorway to his office, his face an unreadable mask. The phone on her desk rang and Kate didn't have to look at the clock to know it was the call he expected. When Richard made no move to return to her office, she answered and asked the princess if they could reschedule the call.

Kate remained standing, and the silence stretched out uncomfortably. The older Prentiss mumbled something, but his son said nothing in response.

Security finally arrived and the two men helped Benedict to his feet—he seemed familiar with both. One of the pair glanced past her to Richard. "Our apologies, Mr. Prentiss. We have a new man on the front desk and he didn't realize protocol."

Richard's gaze never left his father. "Please send a memo around to make sure it doesn't happen again." The security guard nodded and they hustled Benedict out. After they closed the door, Richard glanced at her. "Cancel my five o'clock call. I think I'll have that break after I talk to Frankie."

Kate nodded, she approved but had to maintain her professional demeanor. An assistant wasn't a bodyguard, but her first priority remained his safety—even from himself. "Absolutely, Mr. Prentiss. Can I get you anything else?"

"No and skip the coffee. I'm awake now." His tone made a lie of the words, but he retreated to his office and closed the door.

Kate waited until the light on her phone indicated he was already returning the call to Francesca Grace before pulling out her cell. Dialing a ten-digit number, she waited for the tones to answer and then put in her code. Twenty seconds later a secure operator came on the line. "This is Braddock. I need an expedited background on Prentiss, Benedict, and any open cases, warrants, or judgments."

"Standby." Phone sitting in the cradle of her shoulder, Kate returned to her desk and checked the camera she'd put in Richard's office. The angle was decent and he had a phone pressed to his ear and his mouth moved indicating he spoke, but his head was back and his eyes closed. Shrinking the window and moving it to the upper right-hand corner of her screen, she pulled up the word program and typed in the letters while she waited.

"No open cases or warrants. Several judgments dating back to the early-to mid-90s including three indictments for Ponzi schemes, jail time served from 1994 to 1999, released on parole. Later divorced. Two children from the marriage —Richard Prentiss, attorney, and Barbara, an actress based in London. No close ties to family and at least one, no, make that three open restraining orders."

"From?"

"The children and the ex-wife."

"Understood. Wipe the request, authorization four-alpha-foxtrot-four-two."

"Yes, ma'am. Can I help you with anything else?"

"No." She hung up, rescheduled his five o'clock call, finished the last letter, and printed them. Her cell phone rang—Peterson's name and face flashed up from the screen—and she checked the monitor before answering. "Braddock."

"You put in a request for background information on Benedict Prentiss?" Clipped disapproval hung between every word. Of course, he'd receive notification of every request, even if she had them wiped.

"Yes, sir." She hadn't expected the man to put in an appearance, and she needed more information to make sure she did her job effectively. One day at the office, and she'd already realized that she didn't know near enough about Prentiss's colleagues, clients, and daily interactions. The man headed a law firm with more than two dozen other attorneys.

"He's not involved, leave it alone." Peterson didn't try to explain it.

"Okay, maybe not with the issue at hand, sir, but—"

"Braddock, your assignment is to keep Mr. Prentiss secure. We already know everything we need to about his father. Leave it alone. That's an order."

"Of course, sir." But Peterson had already disconnected the call. Kate pursed her lips. The chain of command existed for a reason—but she was on this assignment alone for the most part. Playing a part was one thing, but protecting him and playing the part required she think ahead. Miranda Keen had provided her with a great deal of information on how to manage Richard's schedule, and his health since apparently he didn't pay as much attention to it as he should.

Classic workaholic. Still, it seemed obtuse to think the only threats to him came from his association with the royal family. Better to be thorough and wrong, than overlook the real threat.

Checking Richard on the monitor, she reached for the phone on her desk and dialed security. "Good afternoon, this is Kate Braddock in Mr. Prentiss's office. We need to conduct a full review of the security protocols governing visitors to the building in general and Mr. Prentiss's floor in particular."

One eye on the screen, she waited to be connected to the head of security. The upgrades couldn't wait and she'd have to apply a little judicious pressure to get the changes she wanted in place before Richard arrived in the office the next day.

He was far too exposed here.

~

INSTEAD OF THIRTY MINUTES, she gave Richard an hour. He'd abandoned his desk and stretched out on the sofa in his oversized office. Shutting off his phone from her desk took three commands. The man's previous PA had a rigid set of useful protocols in place and the detail sheet she'd provided included tips on some of Richard's habits. Switching screens, Kate pulled up a web browser and keyed in the address for a local dress shop.

Finding a dress, shoes and accessories set she liked, she put in a phone call and ordered everything in her size. An extra fee hired a messenger to run it down to the building. Fortunately, she'd been born lucky—store sizes fit exactly as they were supposed to if she stuck to similarly styled outfits. In this case, an off the shoulder sheath that would hit her at mid-thigh. She'd found the invitation for the six-thirty event, two blocks over at a very nice corporate ballroom. Private security would handle admittance and they would have metal detectors. She had a license to carry, but she'd have to leave her gun in the car safe if she didn't want to have to explain the weapon to her protectee. He was far too sharp to just accept on face value she happened to carry a .45.

Mace would be more easily accepted and so would a taser. After all, she was a single woman and lived in a big city.

It would be so much easier if Richard were aware of her assignment, but she'd simply have to muddle through and be creative. Reviewing the rest of Richard's calendar, she checked every event they were scheduled to attend and changed his RSVP on the charity dinner for Thursday to a yes and included a plus one. By the time the messenger arrived, she'd given Richard another twenty minutes to sleep. According to the delightful Miranda's notes, he kept clean shirts, ties and at least one tuxedo in a closet in the private bathroom off his office.

Locking her outer office door and advising the receptionist to divert all but the most pressing of calls to the answering service, Kate changed in her office and used a small mirror to touch up her makeup. Her cell phone buzzed at the ten-minute mark and she checked the message—an advertisement for a twenty percent off deal on all sales made after 6:00 p.m. and before 10:00 p.m.

Familiar with the code, she dialed in then waited.

"He wants to see you this evening," Peterson answered without preamble. "With a report."

"It'll be late. We have an event to attend and a meeting afterward." She kept her gaze on the surveillance camera. Richard was still asleep, an arm slung across his eyes.

"Understood. Call when you're on your way and come up to the security station."

"Yes, sir." They ended the call and Kate took the last few minutes to open the top drawer on her desk halfway, then secured a gun with tape. No bullet in the chamber meant she would need three seconds to get the bullet loaded, but she wanted the backup. Certain no one else would notice it without deliberately looking, she locked the drawer then got her evening bag ready along with a work case and stacked in the letters for Richard to sign.

Letting herself into his office, she knocked quietly on the open door. In her experience, most men didn't like to be woken by a stranger and, despite their six-hour acquaintance, she remained the stranger in the situation. Richard's arm moved away from his eyes and he turned his head.

"You're ready." Displeasure echoed in the drowsy statement. He sat up and swung his feet to the floor. "I said thirty minutes."

"I gave you an hour. I had the dress in the car," she lied easily enough. "I'd forgotten about going to the cleaners. If you want to change, I can make you a cup of coffee and we can go over any notes before we leave."

He scrubbed his hands over his face then nodded, his easy charm muted by sleep and deep thought. He needed a hell of a lot more than just the hour of sleep he'd taken. "Thank you. Excuse me."

While he disappeared into the bathroom, she used the single cup coffee maker in his kitchenette. By the time he returned—hair damp, freshly shaven and wearing a black suit with a deep blue shirt and tie—he looked better. His gaze fell on the cup of coffee steaming on his desk and he tossed her a grateful smile.

"About earlier." He took a drink of the coffee —black with no cream or sugar, she'd have to remember that—and set it down before continuing. "My father will not be something you have to deal with on a regular basis. I am very sorry you had to deal with him at all."

"It's no problem," she told him honestly. She'd already handled the security on that issue. Benedict Prentiss wouldn't get anywhere near him again on her watch.

A lock of dark hair fell over his forehead and she had the urge to stroke it back into place that went beyond the professional.

"Please, let me apologize. You've been swimming like a champion against the riptide. My father is a mean drunk and he can push things. If he shows up again, especially if I'm not here, I want you to alert security and the police immediately. He is *not* your problem and I don't want him to become one."

Nothing in the senior Prentiss's jacket suggested violent offender, but the shadows in Richard's eyes told an entirely different story. "Absolutely, Mr. Prentiss, and speaking of security, they called. Tomorrow morning, a Mr. Hall will present some updated security protocols and deliver the keycards for accessing this floor."

"Keycards?" Richard frowned. He took another swallow of coffee before closing the last two buttons on his shirt and fixing his tie.

"Yes, they are updating the elevators this evening. Only employees and residents will be able to access specific floors without checking in at the security desk below. Visitors will have to sign in and show photo ID. The scan of the ID will then be transmitted to Amelia at the front reception desk and to the personal assistant or secretary for whomever they have an appointment with. We're the ones who will then authorize whether or not they can come up."

A scowl deepened the lines of his forehead. "That's a little overkill, don't you think? We see a lot of clients in this firm."

"Mr. Hall suggested it's been in consideration for some time and they've been preparing to make the necessary changes." Especially after she'd finished speaking to him.

Hardly mollified, Richard frowned. "I'll talk to him. Clients need to feel comfortable coming in here and not like they have to jump through hoops."

That was the last thing she wanted. "I think it will be more comfortable for the clients."

"How so?" His eyebrows raised in challenge. Even fatigued he didn't miss much. That would make her job all the harder as he recovered.

"They will be met in the lobby directly and brought up by an assistant. As it is, we'll be showing each client the type of attention only given to higher paying clients. This levels the playing field, at least on the surface." Would he buy that?

Skepticism filled his expression. "Are you handling me, Ms. Braddock?"

"Absolutely." She had no reason to lie about that. "You have enough on your plate to worry about, I'll make a point of monitoring the new protocols and if there are complaints, we can address it then."

"Fair enough." Richard drained his coffee and

circled out from behind the desk. "Is my tie straight?"

Canting her head to the side, she eyed it critically. "May I?" At his nod, she adjusted it a fraction, then smoothed his collar down. Warmth seeped through the fine material.

"Thank you," but instead of moving away, he met her gaze evenly. Although she wore three-inch heels, he still topped her by a good two inches. She'd always found taller men attractive. "If you wouldn't mind not mentioning my father's visit to anyone."

Odd that he'd make the request considering the non-disclosure, but the hint of vulnerability in his request was deeply personal and had nothing to do with business. "It's no one else's concern." And she meant it. She'd take care of those details. Protectee or not, Richard seemed like a decent guy and deserved some peace of mind.

"Thank you," he said again, then cleared his throat. "Ready? I promise a very nice dinner to say thank you for today."

"No thanks required, but do you mind if I drive?" Her car had bulletproof windows and while Peterson's security had handled the necessary arrangements with Richard's new car following the accident, she was also trained in counter maneuvers should someone try to run him off the road again. If that were the case, well, she'd rather have their safety in her hands. "You can review the letters I typed up and go over tomorrow's calendar. That will make it fresh for later."

"And I'm exhausted." His mouth twisted in a wry smile. "Considering my recent driving history, I can understand the desire and thank you. I'll take you up on it tonight."

Satisfied, she headed back to her office to retrieve her bag and purse.

"But Ms. Braddock?" He stood in the center of his office, hands in his pockets. Gone was any trace of the vulnerable man from before. Instead he studied her with an almost lethal attention.

A purely unprofessional awareness skittered over her. "Yes?"

"Thank you for your concern, but I don't need a nursemaid." The coolness in his tone carried a definite warning.

"I didn't think you did." She lifted her chin, the corners of her mouth tipping upward. They needed to nip this rebellion in the bud. He'd responded to her honesty earlier, hopefully he would again. "However I would be remiss in doing my job if I didn't make sure you were utterly prepared to do yours. I won't baby you and you won't pull any testosterone-fueled crap with me. This works if we're a team, Mr. Prentiss."

His brows crept up and the hard line of his mouth eased. "If we're going to be a *team,* I think you better call me Richard."

"Only if you call me Kate." She didn't care for Kitty, Katie or any of the other nicknames. Though Kate had earned her a fair number of jokes in high school when they'd studied the Cole Porter musical based on *The Taming of the Shrew*.

Warm, masculine laughter echoed from him. "Just Kate?"

Charmed, she grinned. "Yes, just Kate. Thank you. I'll wait for you out here."

"I'm moving." His smile diminished a fraction. "You may not like me much after a few of these events."

"Oh?" She glanced at him as she picked up her purse. "That sounds ominous."

"Dull," he intoned with a half-smile. "Deadly dull."

～

FORTUNATELY, the drive and the event were as dull as Richard predicted. She spent the majority of her attention on memorizing names and faces and making notes after each interaction if Richard asked. At the sixty-minute mark, the lines of fatigue around Richard's eyes worried her, but he was already making excuses for an early departure. They'd even lucked out because the person he'd been scheduled to meet with was at the event. Two birds, one stone. He went quiet once they were back in the car and she concentrated on traffic.

"Did you want me to drop you at your place?" She tested the waters after several minutes of silence. His car was at the office, but if she dropped him off tonight, then she could pick him up in the morning.

"No." He straightened in his seat. "Let's head to The Palm. I promised you dinner and we still have to go over our schedule."

Stubborn man. Her grudging respect for his tenacity continued to grow. "You need reservations for The Palm," she reminded him.

"I have a standing one." He stretched an arm out along the door, the other pressed palm flat against the side of her seat. Regardless of his relaxed posture, he seemed to occupy all the space in the car. "Some relationships stand the test of time."

He didn't expand on his cryptic explanation.

The location and the crowd both set her teeth on edge. She couldn't slip her gun back into her purse with him noticing. A valet took charge of the car at their arrival and Richard carried his bag and hers on their way in. They bypassed the waiting list and the host greeted him by name before showing them directly to a small, private dining room. When he closed the doors, the noise diminished by two-thirds.

Identifying two potential exits, she took the chair that gave her the best vantage of both and angled it so that she would be between Richard and the doors. The second door opened, admitting their waiter.

Richard glanced at her. "Wine? Or would you prefer something else?"

"Water is fine, actually, and a cup of coffee."

"Hmm, I'll take water and coffee as well—make mine decaf, please." The last part he tacked on with a grimace. Loosening the buttons on his

41

suit coat, he sat, then pulled out his digital tablet and the file folders. Kate mirrored his actions.

"Since you eat here often, what do you recommend?" She asked in lieu of looking at the menu. She rarely ate while on the job, but based on his schedule, she would have adjustments of her own to make.

"I usually get the bacon wrapped scallops, a salad, and the swordfish—it's quite excellent. Though the veal marsala or the lamb are nice choices as well."

The wait staff performed efficiently, delivering their drinks and rolls along with his scallops. "Do you mind?" She pointed to the scallops. If he ate here often enough that it was a noticeable habit, poison would be an easy way to go after him.

"Of course not." He nudged the plate toward her and she speared one with a fork. Nothing smelled off, but a good poison wouldn't. Taking a bite, she inspected the flavor and swallowed.

Since most of the actual attacks against the royal family had been physical and Richard's car accident had been lethally direct, poison seemed a far less likely option.

Still, he ate at the restaurant often enough that he could walk right in and his regular schedules made him far easier to clock and target.

When he ordered his swordfish, she murmured she'd take the same. Then they were alone.

"What do you think?" He had reached to take back his plate, but sipped his coffee instead.

"They're quite delicious. You must eat here regularly if they know your order." *Keep it light, Kate.* The only other routine she'd pinned down was his adherence to office hours. The cases he tackled varied. He met clients at their places of business, homes, restaurants and parties as often as he did in his office. Mobility made him a harder target—*which is why they hit in the car.* And why the grand duke had assigned a second unit to shadow him when he was on the road.

She'd picked them out easily, but she'd known what to look for. At least, they kept their distance.

"I used to come in every Tuesday, but not for a few months." Glancing up from his tablet, he nodded to hers. "You sync'd the calendar on both of these?"

Small talk was over, time to get to work. "Before we left the office. I've taken the liberty of suggesting two alterations for the rest of this week. You have appointments in the same area at two different times in the day. If we move the meetings to a central locale, we can actually cover both in less time and that will give you a cleaner afternoon." *And more time to rest.*

He studied the suggested changes, then accepted them. "Clear it with my clients and that looks fine. We don't have to be in court this week, but we will next. I have two briefs that need to be filed Friday—"

"—and the third for Judge Ryan on Monday. Also, I compiled the data for Mikelson v Los Angeles and Officer Randall." She chose the data and flipped it open to the file. She'd earmarked the pages he'd need to complete the brief. "I noticed that one of the depositions hadn't been added to the digital record."

"Whose?" He was already scrolling through the notations.

"Officer LaReaux. He's noted in both Officer Randall's deposition and Mr. Mikelson's as being present during the incident, but we don't have his statement."

Richard pinched the bridge of his nose. "Dammit. Make a note that I need to contact Greg Chambers at the LAPD tomorrow morning, first thing. In fact, send an email to him tonight and get us on his schedule." He paused when the waiter delivered their dinners, letting him serve and exit before continuing. Despite being alone, he dropped his voice. "LaReaux was under investigation in an unrelated matter, but we were asked to hold off on his deposition until IAD concluded the matter."

"And it likely slipped through the cracks during your convalescence." She traded the tablet for her phone. She'd already added the office email, his and hers, to her phone for easy access. She typed up the email with two thumbs and sent it off to the detective he'd mentioned.

They spent their dinner reviewing the open status of his caseload and he gave her a series of cases to pull first thing in the morning. It was after ten when Richard closed his tablet. "Enough for today and..." he glanced at his watch, "...I'll have them call a taxi for me. You should go home and get some sleep. It's going to be an even longer day tomorrow."

"I have to go right past the office on my way home," she lied smoothly. "I can take you to your car." *And after today, I'm going to need a raise.* Being Anna's assistant hadn't required near the same amount of paperwork, emails and schedule management. Richard Prentiss had enough work for three assistants—she needed to manage that *and* watch his back.

He chuckled. "You're in danger of spoiling me, Kate."

"Change your mind at the last minute on any of these plans we've made this evening and we'll see how much I spoil you." Her light tone and hard look had the desired effect—he grinned wider.

"You realize that's a challenge."

"I'd have been disappointed if you didn't see it that way."

Blessedly, the ride back to the office went as quietly and dull as the drive out. She waited until she saw him get in his vehicle and dialed the follow car, miming that her phone had rung when he glanced at her questioningly.

"Rebel is flying solo on the home route and it's twenty-two eighteen." The follow car repeated their acknowledgement and she waited for Richard to back out of his parking space. "Handing off the ball."

Hanging up, she followed him up the ramp to the exit gate and then out onto the street. The black SUV and a second follow car slid out, one ahead and one behind. It took skill to follow a driver by staying in front of them, but since Richard was heading home, they knew where to expect him to go.

Turning in the opposite direction, she had one more stop to make before she could get some sleep. The grand duke wanted a report on his best friend's security situation.

And won't that be an entertaining conversation...

TWENTY-FIVE MINUTES LATER, she found the grand duke waiting for her in Peterson's office. He was alone, and to her surprise, Peterson didn't remain to supervise the discussion. The grand duke was still in his suit, though he'd forgone the tie.

"Thank you for coming by so late, Kate." He waved her toward a chair and settled against the desk rather than sitting. His offer of seating was more an order than a request, so she sat obediently.

"It's not a problem, Your Highness." She clasped her hands together.

"Richard hired you." It wasn't a question, but concern furrowed the grand duke's brow. The man transformed control freak into dignified art. "How is he?"

"He's well." It was a non-committal answer, but their brief acquaintance said a great deal about Richard's tenacity. He didn't give in to the suggestion of weakness.

"That I know, but how is he really? What is

his schedule like? Do we need to try and lighten his workload? Should I bully him into taking more time off?" The grand duke's European accent sharpened and he enunciated each word with care.

"Your Highness, you'll have to forgive me. The parameters of my assignment are clear. Mr. Prentiss is my *protectee*, I cannot discuss the behavior of my protectee. Not even with you." Unfortunately, that answer didn't satisfy him.

"Richard is my dearest, oldest friend." If he thought repeating the same information to her would get him what he wanted He was wrong.

"I understand, Your Highness." And she did. She understood the lengths to which he would go to protect those he considered his. He'd hired her twice now to do the exact same job. "I must still say no."

As a man few people ever denied, he really didn't like her telling him no.

So he called in Peterson.

Thankfully, the security chief backed her.

It was after midnight by the time she left the tower and almost one before she fell face-first into her bed.

5:00 a.m. came too swiftly, but she lunged out of bed and did a five-mile run on the treadmill before showering and heading to the office. She wanted to be in place before Richard and she wanted a good look at his fellow attorneys.

She really did need a raise. This undercover shit blew.

THE NEXT SEVERAL days mirrored the first in terms of workload. Needing the additional time to begin building profiles of his employees, Kate arrived at the office every morning before seven. If she didn't, Richard beat her. In addition to Richard, his firm included a dozen senior associates and nearly two dozen junior associates. As the only named partner, Richard had the final say on all their cases—a fact he seemed to take to heart.

"What are you doing?" Richard's arrival had been announced by his security tail, so she had time to put away her research notes and meet his inquiry with a faint smile.

"Catching up with He Who Does So Much." Rising, she preceded him to his office door and opened it. "I set up your coffee maker, you just have to hit brew. Your morning meds are on the desk. I've pulled the two briefs you wanted to review. The Wilkinson deposition has been rescheduled, and Mr. Grange's secretary called. Mr. Grange would like you to sit in on a phone call this afternoon for Mr. Voldakov if you have the time."

And most of that was in the last fifteen minutes. She'd changed her mind, Richard Prentiss had enough work for four assistants. That she had to oversee his security simply added to the load.

His cell phone rang before he could respond. Richard pulled it out of his pocket and answered it with a thumb swipe. "Morning, Armand, you're at your desk earlier than I am."

Ignoring his conversation, Kate took his brief case and carried it over to the desk and started the coffee going before withdrawing a bottle of water from the fridge. She opened it, and put it on the desk right next to his meds and pointed at them while he continued talking.

Richard paused and covered the phone. "I'll take them in a minute."

"No, you'll take them now because His Highness will talk business for at least twenty minutes, then you'll discuss his upcoming wedding before you segue into his management plans for the rest of the family and you'll forget to take them before the deposition you wanted to sit in on with one of the junior associates." She folded her arms and stared at him, daring him to deny it.

"Give me a moment, Armand." Richard hit a button on his phone and set it down. After opening the bottles one at a time, he took the meds he was supposed to and washed them down with water. "Happy?" He eyed her, his expression more fitting a recalcitrant six-year-old than a grown man.

"Did you eat this morning?" she countered. In her limited experience over the last four days, the man didn't eat unless someone dropped a meal on him during a meeting.

"I have a call," he told her pointedly.

"I'll take that as a no and order you up a steak bagel breakfast sandwich. It will be here in thirty minutes. Wrap up with His Highness before then and I'll let you have another cup of coffee with your breakfast." Amused by his blink of surprise, she put away his prescription bottles then delivered his coffee before retreating out of his office, aware of his stare the whole time.

The man needed a keeper.

After placing the breakfast order, she checked her surveillance on his office—he was seated behind the desk and had the cell phone back to his ear. Satisfied, she pulled out her notes on the attorneys in his office—so far they all proved to be as clean and honorable as the man who'd hired them.

CHAPTER 3
RICHARD

The next week sped past and he not only got ahead of his cases, but managed to close two—including Leonard v. Johnson.

Blake had come through in spades. Leonard's last continuance had been filed to allow the man to take a trip to Vegas where he'd not only partied, but ended up in jail on charges of public intoxication. Armed with enough evidence to debunk the majority of Leonard's claims, Richard had met with the other man's attorney and the lawsuit had been withdrawn.

Kate had gone with him to deliver the news to Brett Johnson and the older man had nearly wept.

He liked winning his *pro bono* cases, but Richard would savor the Johnson victory for some time to come. Men like Leonard, who wanted to take advantage of other people's misfortune made him sick. Richard wasn't ashamed to admit he couldn't have handled the sheer volume without Kate.

She'd smoothed over all the rough edges, rolled with the changes, and found more efficient ways to pack his schedule in so he could maximize his time. But he'd also noticed the hour-long windows she gave him in the late mornings *and* late afternoons—windows of time where he could rest his eyes, or at least take a break.

She *was* handling him. His unflappable assistant handled him like a professional.

"You make that sound like a bad thing." Armand filled two crystal tumblers with ice and added water.

"It's odd. Miranda micromanaged my schedule, but not me. Kate, she's different. She makes changes, but only afterward does it seem like it's my idea. The funny thing is that I didn't realize it until today. She's good." Uncertain whether he should be impressed or irritated, Richard decided to go with the former over the latter.

Armand laughed. "Enjoy it. Anna's been talking to Peterson again, and Gretchen. I have three nights in each week. No events." The genial tone declared the prince had no problems with his fiancée's decision making.

"Have you two finally set a date?" Richard accepted the glass and stretched his legs out in front of him. They were supposed to be going over the latest corporation paperwork, but neither man reached for the stacks in front of them.

"Fall. She wants an autumn wedding on her parents' farm." The smug grin couldn't have anything to do with the Middle American, rustic setting Anna desired. It was about as far from European royalty as the couple could get.

"Have you told your mother?" Richard lifted his brows. The matriarch highly approved of her future daughter-in-law, but he doubted she'd be as delighted with a hayfield wedding.

"Oh, that was my third call." Armand laughed. "I had to tell Sebastian and George first, so they would have time for duck and cover."

"What about your great-aunts?" The dowager duchesses were a canny old pair. Richard made a point of never being in their line of sight if they were expected. Unfortunately, Armand's wedding would make them unavoidable —particularly since he would be best man.

"Bring a date, unless you want to be Rose's latest conquest," Armand advised. His royal cousin had earned her share of notoriety since reaching her majority and she was wild as her twin sister was calm. "Hell, bring two. I'll get you some numbers."

Unable to cover a grimace, Richard considered whom he could take to the official wedding. "How much of a circus are you two planning?"

"A small wedding actually. This one will be very intimate, family and friends only." Which immediately eliminated about three-quarters of the people Armand did business with, and it wouldn't make them happy.

Unhappy business partners meant meetings to soothe ruffled feathers and more. He'd have to plan ahead for that eventuality.

"You're never going to pull that off, not after the press already had a taste with Alyx's wedding." Armand's long-lost cousin had made a splashy, royal debut and her wedding to a California software developer had turned into a public relations dream come true—right down to the royal attendants at an American wedding. The ridiculous feeding frenzy that followed had continued to dog Armand and his brothers. Rekindling his relationship with his college sweetheart kept the machine so well fed, Sebastian and George might never come out of hiding.

"We might." Armand's sly grin suggested he'd already found a way to resolve the issue. "We'll be announcing a spring wedding during our late summer fundraisers. First in casual conversation and then with an official announcement when we award the first Princess Alyxandretta Scholarships."

"Spring. The press will start digging to see where you're having the wedding." It might work. They'd be looking in the most logical of places—France, Norway and Los Angeles. "Who's handling the wedding planning?"

"Anna and her mother. They will do all the ordering and use multiple vendors from around the country. They've already started. A small shipment here, a large shipment there—very innocuous and always timed with a charity event. If all goes as planned, we'll be married with just forty or fifty of our closest friends."

"That's a perfect blend of ingenuity and deviousness," Richard mused, impressed.

"All Anna." Pride filled Armand's tone.

Richard approved. He'd had to pick up the pieces when Anna had left Armand all those years before and something inside of his friend had changed, broken and hardened. Armand hadn't laughed as loudly or smiled as bright. His humor had taken a slightly darker bent and he'd thrown himself into work and foundation projects. In recent months, Richard had seen his old friend re-emerging.

Hell, from his hospital bed and hopped up on medication, Richard had enjoyed a front row seat to the conflict Armand fought with himself over bringing Anna back into his life. Thank God he'd finally forgiven her, and more—fallen in love with her again. Richard wasn't a romantic—far from it. But Anna and Armand gave him hope.

They fit each other. After all the pain they'd put each other through, they'd found a way to be together, and Armand appeared happier than he'd been in years.

Win-win-win as far as Richard was concerned, even if it did mean a hell of a lot more work.

"Well as much fun as picking colors and plate patterns would be, we should go through all of this." Sparing a glance at his watch, Richard sighed. "In about forty-two minutes, Kate will poke her head in here to gently remind me that I have a dinner engagement at six."

Armand didn't disguise his amusement. He was all smiles today. "You have your assistant's timing down that perfect?"

"Hey, you sent her to me. I figured it had something to do with keeping a royal schedule." Richard appreciated the hell out of Kate's dedication—she never failed to pull him out of his distractions and always seemed to know exactly what to say to get him moving. He'd discovered that if he occasionally dug his heels in, he could make her frown.

And he liked the feel of her biting wit.

He flipped open the top folder and eyed the language. In addition to opening up new revenue streams, the contracts would include the first European awarded contracts for Spherecast Technologies, courtesy of three corporations that Armand maintained the controlling interest in. Both men wanted to make sure Daniel's assets— and thus Alyx's—were wholly protected as he sliced into a market that had formally been closed to him.

"I've read the first two and didn't find a problem." Armand sobered. "It's the third one I have some questions about."

"Reading." He ignored the urge to hurry. Richard had faith in Armand's business savvy, but it was Richard's job to protect the family's legal interests—and that now included any negotiations with the princess's husband's company. Not that anyone would tell Daniel or Alyx until they'd made sure all the *t*'s were crossed and the *i*'s dotted—that was how Armand worked.

It's always easier to ask for forgiveness than it is for permission.

"Do you know how to play golf?" They were on their way to his club. Richard had swung by her apartment spontaneously to pick her up. He hadn't been sure whether to be disappointed or pleased to find her dressed and ready for the day when he knocked on her door at 8:00 a.m. on a Sunday morning. Kate was always so put together, so in charge, he hadn't called ahead on purpose. He'd wanted a peek at the *real* her. Instead, she wore jeans, a golden polo shirt and a pair of comfortable running shoes.

"I'm familiar with the game." It was the most casual he'd seen her since she came to work for him. Though he'd developed a certain fondness for her cocktail dresses. The woman possessed a killer pair of legs. "Although, I'm not entirely certain why you felt the need to conduct business during your tee time."

He hadn't. Picking her up had been an impulse, one he hadn't put a lot of thought into. They'd worked in each other's back pockets for the better part of two weeks. Today should have been her first day off. "Business happens as often on the golf course as off of it." But he still needed some validity for her presence. "And I didn't realize I shared tee time with Walsinger, Kravitts, and Bing."

"Bing?" She shot him a questioning look. "You don't have a client named Bing."

"True. I don't have one named Walsinger or Kravitts either."

"But you handled contracts with their respective companies for the grand duke and Kravitts actually wants the contracts in the EU that you and the grand duke are planning to hand over to Spherecast Technologies." She flipped her ponytail back. The gorgeous length fell to below her shoulder blades.

Until he'd seen it that morning, he hadn't realized how often she pinned her hair up or just how much of it she possessed. The sensuous length made him think of a sunshine waterfall, all shimmering gold, shot through with tawny streaks of flax.

"I handed you those contracts yesterday." He hadn't shared any of the details of his meetings with Armand until he'd been ready to have the grand duke finalize them. Following their meeting the afternoon before, they'd returned to the office and he'd handed her the copies to enter digitally.

All U.S. based parties would be in his office Tuesday morning to authorize signings, ensure notarization, and then transmit to the office of his Brussels' counterpart for signatures in Europe. Coordination and discretion were the two weapons they had in their arsenal to make sure the deal went through smoothly.

News would break in the European business markets first and ripple across. It would be a hell of a week, but they'd worked through mountains of regulations on both sides to create the perfect soft entry for *Spherecast*. Voldakov had the knowledge and the skill to take that lead and run with it.

And Armand gets to protect his cousin's interests at the same time and maybe absolve his personal guilt over her orphaning.

Though he wasn't to blame for it, Armand took Alyx's time in foster care personally. He wanted to do everything he could to make up for it whether it was his fault or not.

The man didn't know how to draw personal lines when it came to the lives of those he loved. His devotion to family was an admirable trait, but it bordered on interference at times.

"Richard?" Kate's voice held a sharp note and he jerked a glance toward her, then the road.

"What?"

"You missed your turn for the club back there." She pointed with her thumb over her shoulder and he slowed down enough to glance back.

"Son of a bitch—sorry, I was distracted." He swung into the right-hand lane and completed a series of turns to head back to the golf course.

"Apparently, and yes, you handed me the contracts yesterday. I made sure they were scanned in and correct before we left the office. They're in the passcoded dropbox so we can access as needed."

"And you read them? Enough to recognize the names?" That counted as impressive even by the standards she'd performed since hiring her.

A shrug met his inquiry and she pointed at the gated drive for the club. "Don't miss it again."

Richard followed the drive and found his parking slot. Putting the car in park, he turned in the seat, curious as hell, to look at his assistant. "Spill."

Her attention wasn't on him, however. Instead she scanned the club parking area, not that there was much to see, though the parking lot was over half full. A lot of the locals preferred the earlier tee times before the Hollywood types hit the greens. She pushed up her sunglasses to rest on top of her head and swung her gaze back to him at the order. "Excuse me?"

"You heard me." He searched her face. He had the oddest sensation of seeing her for the first time. Her soft brown eyes were actually hazel in the morning sun, with hints of gold and deeper green. She didn't wear cosmetics beyond a gloss for lipstick and a hint of eye shadow. "Spill. Speed reading? Eidetic memory? How are you picking up all of this so fast and remembering it so clearly?"

"Reading is a fairly basic skill. I learned that in kindergarten." Her lashes swept down, then back up. The corner of her mouth curved with the barest hint of a smile. And there she went, trying to manage him again—by misdirecting his attention. "One I apparently excel at."

It was damn subtle and, as much as it amused him, he still wanted an answer. "A five-year-old couldn't process one seventy-five-page contract, much less three in the two hours you had them prior to the dinner we attended."

"What makes you think I wasn't reading them at dinner?" Challenge flared in her eyes.

Richard snorted. "I would have noticed your digital tablet and that green dress left you nowhere to hide it."

Her smile grew and she held up her right hand. Her phone faced him and the contract appeared when she swiped her thumb across the screen. "But I had my phone."

"Damn." He hit the steering wheel. "So that's what you were doing when I asked you to dance." Her attention had been on the plate of salad, though he could have sworn she watched the room more than looked down. She always seemed to be aware of everything going on around her.

"It's merely a matter of dividing my attention." Another careless shrug. "As for the memory, I'm trained in observation. I'd hardly make a worthwhile assistant if I couldn't identify, assess and remember key details."

"Like names?" He nodded slowly. "That makes sense." But he wasn't buying it. Kate Braddock presented him with an enigma. "So how long do you retain these key pieces of data? I mean you worked with Anna for months. Can you name the top donors for the scholarship fund?"

He shut off the engine and opened the car door, stepping out into the sunshine. Unsurprisingly, she exited immediately and circled the car to meet him. She was good at that too—he'd thought it was because he'd been coming off his convalescence, that she always kept a step ahead of him. But he'd begun to suspect it was left over from traveling in Anna's security detail.

"I could." She slid her phone into the back pocket of her jeans and adjusted her purse on her shoulder. She carried a very practical bag, nothing frilly, but the one time he'd picked it up to hand it to her the weight had impressed him.

"And they are?" He motioned to her to proceed, then opened his trunk to retrieve his golf clubs.

"I said I *could* tell you, not that I would." The corners of her mouth turned up into an amused grin and she glanced around.

"It's hardly privileged information. I could look the names up." He represented the fund.

"I was under a nondisclosure agreement that remains binding whether I work for Miss Novak or not." She spared him another wry look. "A nondisclosure I believe you drafted."

"Hmm, hoisted by my own legal acumen." Richard set his club bag on the ground and closed the trunk. "Well played, Kate. Well played."

"Thank you, sir." She grinned and that twinkle gleamed in her eyes.

Loosening the handle on his club bag, he tugged it along and motioned her to move ahead of him as she would likely do anyway. "I said well-played. You haven't won yet."

"Oh?" She glanced at him over her shoulder. "Are we keeping score in this game?"

"We are now."

~

THEY MANAGED the first five holes in relative peace and quiet, addressing only the most pleasant of topics. Bing, as it turned out, was not someone Richard knew at all. He'd expected an attorney or financial advisor and instead Bruno Bing turned out to be an actor and the brother-in-law of Kravitts—and wholly uninterested in the game.

Bing never took his attention off Kate.

"The problem we're running into with this latest set of regulations from the EU is narrowing the market share." Walsinger walked a half circle around the tee, his gaze on the hole 192 yards away. The man could never just take a shot. He had to cozy up to it like a woman he wanted to pick up in a bar. "First, it was just the German trades. Now France and Spain are adding in changes and adjustments. Belgium suggested three more and the U.K.—they're proving intractable on Atlantic crossover."

This wasn't Richard's first rodeo. Walsinger wanted Richard to talk to Armand and grease the wheels for him.

Bing stood off to the right, his mouth moving and his hand on Kate's shoulder. To her credit, she glanced at the actor once and moved a half step away forcing his hand to drop off of her. She didn't seem to pay him any attention, instead she watched Walsinger and his shot and then looked over the landscape.

What the hell is he talking to her about?

Bing did all the talking. Kate hadn't said anything that Richard'd noticed.

Kravitts folded his arms. "Just take the shot, Harvey, so the rest of us can play. We've got folks two holes behind us and they'll be asking to play through if you take much longer."

Walsinger paused to give Kravitts a baleful look and then positioned himself, lining up his club, but he was nowhere near ready to swing. Richard ignored the theatrics of the shot to check on Kate. Bing touched her, again. Irritation flared along his nerve endings and he locked gazes with his assistant. He hadn't brought her with him to be pawed by that clown.

Brows up, he flicked a look to Bing and back to her. The corner of her mouth curved and she crossed her eyes, but gave a subtle shake of her head. She didn't need him to intercede.

"Don't you think our long-standing history should count for something? My company has maintained three factories in Germany since 1947," Walsinger continued to grumble and twice he worked his arm, testing his angle.

Richard waited a beat for him to play before replying. "I think reminding the oversight committees that your company took advantage of post-war rebuilding to get a financial foothold in their country that funneled money out instead of in wouldn't be prudent."

Scowling, the older man pointed his golf club at him. "That's not a particularly generous description of how my company does business."

"It's not a particularly generous market, Harvey, and you are free to take the advice or not." He didn't flinch at the anger in the other man's eyes, no matter how irrational. Harvey Walsinger knew how to cut a deal; temper tantrums were not typically a part of them. Something else was up.

"Let's keep playing and allow cooler heads to prevail. We have a week until the consortium hands out its approvals for the next fiscal year's contracts. Plenty of time to make this work." Kravitts swept in with a conciliatory gesture. His gaze, however, remained fixed on Walsinger until Harvey lowered his club and grunted an assent.

"Kate." Richard didn't look at her, waiting while Walsinger and Kravitts headed out to take the next shot. Arriving at his elbow, Kate lifted a brow, but her tag-a-long hovered right behind her. Pausing, Richard eyed him. "The play is that way." He continued to stare and Bing raised his hands in a mild offer of surrender that his eyes promised he had no interest in paying. He followed the other two men.

After Bilbo Bing was out of earshot, Kate glanced at him. "Do you want me to call your investigator to find out what is going on between those two?"

"Yes, text him. I assume you have the number —and then check the SEC filings tomorrow morning." They knew about the upcoming consortium announcement. No matter how quiet and low key he played it, Kravitts was fishing for an inside lead.

"Walsinger isn't your problem." Of course

she'd noticed it too. Kravitts had requested the golf game.

"I know. What does Cousin It want?" The reference to the actor's shaggy flop of blond hair earned an arrested smile from his assistant.

"An introduction to Her Royal Highness." Kate didn't miss a beat. She had her phone out and quick typed the text to Mitch. "I think he's supposed to be charming you, but he has a thing for breasts."

Pivoting to face her, a quiet anger simmered to life in his blood. "Is he being inappropriate?"

"No, I think he's going for charismatic or seductive." The offhand dismissal in her remark didn't alleviate his concern. Message sent, she tucked her phone into her back pocket and glanced behind them and then ahead to Kravitts taking his shot.

"About your breasts?" He wanted to be absolutely clear when he dealt with the man.

"Well, it started with my ass and moved to my breasts. I assume my lips will be the next topic of conversation if he can get his gaze above the neckline. For some reason he seems to be under the misapprehension that detailing his varied knowledge of anatomy will somehow coax forth an invitation to meet Her Royal Highness." Kate shrugged. "He's harmless. Ignore him. Kravitts, however, is not."

Kravitts definitely wasn't. The man had an agenda, but he'd dealt with sharks before. "I'll take care of Bing. You don't have to put up with that crap."

Club bag in hand he started forward, irked beyond measure with the sleaze. Kate's hand touched his arm and he paused mid-step. "Richard, seriously. Ignore him. He's harmless."

"He keeps touching you." An unfamiliar violence surged through him. He didn't care what the other man's motivations were, Kate was not an option for manipulation or abuse.

Her expression fluctuated, surprise appearing briefly before it shuttered away and his unflappable assistant reappeared. "I didn't realize that bothered you. I'll take care of it."

"Of course it bothers me." Did she think it wouldn't? He ignored the other three men who had begun to look back at them impatiently. They were waiting for Richard to finish his shot. They could wait. "You're my assistant. I bring you along for your brain, not so others can paw at you like a piece of meat." Their behavior bugged the hell out of him. It was one thing for businessmen to try and use Richard to get to Armand and his family, he wouldn't allow them to use Kate that way.

The corner of her mouth turned up and Kate inclined her head. "I didn't think you had, but duly noted. Thank you."

"You're welcome." Still aggravated, he glanced down the fairway toward the others. Kravitts was using Walsinger to badger him and his brother-in-law to pester Kate, which meant he wanted Richard's attention divided and elsewhere. "Keep an eye on Kravitts, and if Cousin It touches you again, I'm going to break his hand."

Another flicker of surprise—apparently his candor *had* startled her. She brushed his forearm, a light caress, soothing and electric in one. The unexpected sensation lanced through his temper. "He won't. No worries. It's your turn and they're impatient. I don't think Kravitts is done with his show yet."

Grateful to be on the same wavelength, Richard focused his attention on the men waiting for them. Had Miranda ever suffered this type of treatment? He couldn't recall—but then he'd never brought Miranda to the course with him.

So why had he brought Kate?

They'd wanted a casual game, to curry favor and win points so they could wheedle a deal, or at least open the talks to one. It was how business was done in higher circles—meetings at the club, a game of golf, a drink afterward and the promise of potential business. A little oily and sometimes more than a little corrupt, but how men played at these levels. But Kravitts should have leashed his pet actor and never involved Kate; it just pissed Richard off.

~

KATE

After the last hole, Kate had ridden with Richard back to the clubhouse. He'd left her to wait while he vanished into the locker room. She leaned against the wall. After watching him handle the three men on the course, she wasn't worried about them in the locker room with him, but she couldn't say the same for anyone else using the club.

Though the club was approved by Peterson because the grand duke often used it alongside Richard, so she suspected they had an inside man, or three, on the staff.

Walsinger appeared in the doorway and gave her a pleasant nod before heading deeper into the club. No sign of Richard or of Kravitts and his little puppy dog, Bing, either.

The next fifteen minutes passed in agonizing slowness. Spending her day off at the golf course hadn't been on her agenda, but when Richard showed up at her door without preamble or warning she'd agreed.

Not that I needed to, and I could certainly have made a case for staying home.

So why hadn't she?

Pushing aside that thought, she glanced at her watch. What was taking him so long? Worry ratcheted the tension in her spine. Maybe he'd taken a shower—not that he'd seemed overly warm from the game, but then she didn't know about his club habits.

"I'm sure it was a misunderstanding." Kravitts's voice echoed down the hallway, alerting her a second before the man himself appeared alongside Richard. Bing followed, a half-frown on his face.

"Well then, clarify the part for me that I misunderstood," Richard said smoothly, but something dangerous lurked in his too polite tone.

"You scheduled a tee time with me to discuss business, but invited along Walsinger—a man you know will never be allowed at the table—and your brother-in-law who is only suited for a blackjack table. You then avoid any presumptive discussion of business while letting Walsinger hurl insults. In the meanwhile, your brother-in-law spent the majority of his time hitting on my assistant in an attempt to get information on Her Royal Highness, knowing full well that's a breach of ethics and privilege at this club."

Both men had gone very still during Richard's recitation and Kravitts shot Bing an angry look before his expression smoothed. "I didn't see your assistant rebuffing him or I would have certainly said something—"

Richard lifted a hand. "I'm sorry, do you mean to imply that you have no problem with your brother-in-law pawing a woman and making sexual overtures during a *business* meeting—or any other kind of meeting, for that matter—provided she doesn't complain?"

The temperature around them plummeted. Kate wasn't the only one who noticed the icy force of Richard's temper. Bing paled and actually took a step back, but Kravitts struggled to find a response, mouth gaping like a fish.

"Of course not, you have my apologies. It won't happen again." Without another word, Kravitts turned and seemed to notice her for the first time. With a brusque nod, he hustled his brother-in-law away and left her alone with Richard.

She'd known Richard had been less than en-thused about Bing's behavior on the greens, not that it bothered her. The wanna-be-actor had presented all the danger of a fly, and only twice the nuisance because she couldn't just swat him. But damn if Richard hadn't shown his teeth.

No wonder he had the reputation he did—all good looks, smooth charm and the vicious bite to back it up.

"Lunch?" he asked with a charming smile, one that reached his eyes. Maybe the man did need a keeper, but after that display she found herself more intrigued by the man behind the attorney's mask.

"I'd love some." What other secrets did he keep so expertly hidden?

The bartender set the bottle of beer on a napkin and picked up the ten-dollar bill she'd left for him. His security arrived ahead of them and she watched via the mirror on the bar back as they walked the room.

Quiet, high-end and exclusive, the Felicity was not a downtown hotspot and, between the hours of nine and ten at night, it was damn near dull. Patrons picked up at ten-thirty when the local theaters lowered their curtains. Until then, the very public venue provided an ideal backdrop for an "accidental" encounter.

"Ms. Braddock." Armand Dagmar, Grand-Control-Freak and prince-pain-in-the-ass took the seat next to her.

"Your Highness," she murmured quietly. They really needed to stop meeting like this. *Seriously.* "You wanted to see me?" She rolled the bottle between her palms and refrained from taking a drink or tacking on the *again* on the end of the sentence. An evening kicking back in a chair with a beer in one hand and some mindless action flick on the television sounded good, but in the three weeks since she'd taken the job as Richard Prentiss's assistant, she hadn't had more than five consecutive hours to herself and she needed every one of those for sleep.

"Yes and thank you for taking the time this evening. Where does Richard think you are?" As tempted as she was to tell him that Richard knew she was here reporting to his best friend, she decided against being glib.

"Does it matter?" The grand duke's constant need for hands on reports threatened the operation, but apparently, he didn't care.

"I suppose not." Armand accepted the tumbler with amber liquid in it and the bartender retreated to a discreet distance. "How is he doing?"

"He's exactly as he appears." Discomforted by the questions, she chanced a direct look at the grand duke. She'd had a front row seat to his near self-destruct with Anna. He was a man who wore his responsibilities like a hair shirt, but more—he was overprotective of those he loved. They'd already gone through a few rounds of this her first day on the job. Maybe she could cut him some slack. "And he's secure currently, as secure as we can make him, Your Highness."

Concern deepened the grooves around the grand duke's mouth. "Peterson's kept you up to date on the current chatter?"

"Following the consortium announcement? Yes, sir." Kravitts continued to maneuver to be a power player, but Richard had begun to string him along. He'd even taken a particular glee in it after the day on the course. "Peterson also said that security for the Voldakovs was doubled as a result. But none of that chatter includes Mr. Prentiss." Though that seemed too simple. She'd continued to work her way through the attorneys at his firm and their previous caseloads, but it was taking forever. Richard continued to juggle a caseload that would make an associate attorney blanch, much less the major shareholder in his own firm, he handled the work—not to mention the projects he refused to allow her to sit in on. Impressively well.

Leaning forward, the prince clasped his hands together on the bar. "Ms. Braddock—Kate —how is *he* doing?"

She understood the question and, while she sympathized, she gave him a brief albeit regretful smile. "As I told you, I'm not permitted to discuss the behavior of my protectee."

"And as I told you, you work for me." The first time the grand duke cornered her on this issue, she'd had Peterson to back her up. Since then, Peterson was never present. The grand duke really didn't like being told no.

"Yes, Your Highness, and you hired me to protect Mr. Prentiss, and before that, you charged me with the protection of your fiancée. In pursuit of these goals, I have been employed by both. I would no sooner betray her secrets, than I will his." They really needed to nip this in the bud. "Whether Mr. Prentiss knows I am his bodyguard or not, I can't protect him if he feels he has to do things behind my back and so I am not permitted to discuss the behavior of my protectee."

"You realize I can replace you." It was an empty threat.

"Your Highness, I don't discuss you or your family or Mr. Prentiss with anyone. You can obviously replace me. That is absolutely at your discretion. But you'll choose one of these men around you or someone like them. They will not give you the answers any more than I will. I am happy, however, to meet with you regularly to tell you no if it brings you peace of mind."

Whatever the grand duke might have said in response ended when the door to the street opened and Richard entered.

Adrenaline flooded her system and she picked up her beer and took a long drink. She'd have about twenty-five minutes to find food before the alcohol on an empty stomach messed with her reactions, but they needed this to look like a casual encounter. Two other familiar faces entered with Richard.

"Alyxandretta." Armand rose smoothly and opened his arms to embrace the flame-haired princess.

"Okay, I adore you and accept you as family, but can you please just call me Alyx?" The woman laughed as she hugged him. Her blond husband wrapped an arm around his wife when she stepped back, and grasped Armand's hand in a firm grip.

Richard gave her a curious look. "Didn't expect to see you here."

Because it would be far more noticeable if she pretended to not notice any of them, Kate stood and turned her attention to all the new arrivals and gave Richard a chagrinned smile. Saluting him with her beer bottle in lieu of a greeting, she chuckled. "Busted."

"So I see." Amusement softened the note of curiosity in his gaze. "Join us? We ran into each other at the theater... Alyx, Daniel, you remember my new assistant, Kate." Fortunately, neither had been aware of her position as security for Anna Novak, only as her assistant.

"Of course I do." Alyx tossed her a friendly grin. "Anna misses you terribly at the foundation, but I can understand why Richard lured you away."

"He didn't."

"I didn't." Richard chuckled and they all moved to one of the larger tables in the back. Security filtered in until the population in the bar had nearly tripled. The prince, princess, and Prentiss were all in the same place.

"Actually, Richard found himself in dire straits and I persuaded Anna to part with Ms. Braddock's very capable services to help out an old friend." The prince delivered the explanation smoothly and distracted the couple by asking about the show.

Arm draped casually over the back of her chair, Richard leaned closer. "I thought you were dropping off papers with Judge Harding?"

"I did." She kept her voice low. "And then I thought I would sneak out for a beer while you went to the musical."

"You could have joined me," he reminded her, because he had invited her.

"I thought you said it was pleasure, not business and—" Kate shifted her chair, and glanced back at the entrance, "—what happened to your date?"

"Oh, that woman." Alyx perked up and grinned. "Poor Richard, his date stood him up. That's why Daniel and I rescued him."

Stood up? Kate made a mental note to check on the woman. The waitress delivered a round of drinks.

"She was unavoidably detained." Richard shrugged, though for once his poker face wasn't in evidence. "She didn't miss much." But there was something in the way his gaze flicked to her. He'd invited Kate to join him earlier in the day, but she'd seen the name Diane Fowler on the calendar and reminded him—Kate shook her head. Classic workaholic forgetting he needed balance in his life. Enjoying his company each day in the office while she also provided him with security didn't mean she needed to police his romantic life—or lack thereof. If it had been a business event, fine, but he'd not indicated anything of the kind. In fact, he'd appeared genuinely surprised when she'd reminded him of his date. She suspected he'd forgotten the engagement altogether. So perhaps his date had as well.

"I really wanted to like it." Alyx propped her

chin on her hand. Despite her royal heritage and the acknowledged place in the Andraste family, Alyx Voldakov remained true to her American upbringing.

"That's because you wanted to play the part of Esmerelda," her husband teased and she stuck her tongue out at him. The playful, easy affection was a pleasant distraction from the undercurrents at the table. Richard stopped watching her and focused his attention on Armand. Both men spoke in such low undertones that she would have to lean toward them to hear what they were saying.

Not that their topic was any of her business.

"I think I would have been brilliant and the show would be sold out." Alyx's mock petulance gave way to another wide grin. "Did you see the text Victor sent during the second act?"

"Bland, pedestrian and insulting were the politest words he used." Daniel shook his head and slanted a look at Kate. "You were smart to turn Richard's offer down, Kate. If he makes you go to one of those, ask for a raise first."

She chuckled. "If I can handle eighteen holes of golf, I think I can handle a dreadfully dull show." Awareness slicked over her. She had Richard's attention once more, but she kept her gaze on Alyx and Daniel. It went against the grain to have her back to the door, but she knew every one of the five men stationed around the room. They were all good.

"It wasn't dull." Alyx grimaced. "It was painful."

79

Another round of laughter and the waitress returned. "Yes, let's eat." The prince glanced around at all of them. "Anna is with Penny and I'm not allowed back at the tower for another two hours."

That was her cue to excuse herself. "Actually, if you will all forgive me..." She rose and so did all three men at the table. Impeccable manners, all of them. Her gaze clashed with Alyx's and the woman's amusement was palpable. "I have a few items to prepare for tomorrow's agenda."

"Oh, now that's not fair," Alyx protested before she could take a step. "Richard is staying, so you should be able to as well."

"I don't mind if you join us for a meal, Kate." Richard gave her an odd look. "I looked at the calendar before I left, we don't have any early meetings or court appearances. You've dropped off the documents with the judge."

"Maybe she doesn't want to have dinner with her boss." Daniel, at least, seemed to be on her side.

"But if she goes and you three begin discussing business or sports, I may die of boredom." Alyx steepled her hands together. "Besides, you haven't finished your beer. You should stay and order the largest steak they have."

"Yes, Ms. Braddock, you should feel perfectly welcome to join us." The prince added his weight to the tables being turned against her. Socializing with a protectee was off limits. However, she couldn't play that card and Armand's smug smile told her he was well aware of the fact.

"Come on, Kate. Sit down, have dinner and, I promise, no work tonight." Richard took hold of the back of her chair and his voice dropped to a lower note. "Please, have dinner with us."

"You know, speaking of work." Daniel looked thoughtful. "I've been meaning to talk to you two about— Ow." He rubbed his arm and grinned at his wife. "Fine, no work."

Richard gave her a sly look, one that spoke of shared secrets. "Come on, Kate, it's easier to say yes and then we bill them for the hours later when they forget and start talking business anyway."

More laughter met the droll statement and she couldn't hold back a grin. Uncertain whether she was more uncomfortable with the invite or that she *wanted* to stay, she let Richard coax her back into her seat. "Fine, but the first mention of under par, over par or contract language and all bets are off."

"Oh, I like you." Alyx held out her wine glass and clinked it to Kate's beer bottle. Beside her, Richard's attention remained almost laser focused on her and every hair on her body stood up and took notice.

This is a mistake.

~

ONE HOUR TURNED into three and Richard insisted on seeing her home, until she'd pointed out he'd shared a limo with Alyx and Daniel to the bar and sent his own car home. By the time they'd reached that realization, however, the royals and their vehicles had departed, which was how she ended up driving him to his place.

Fortunately, she'd switched to water after her beer and the fish and chips she'd ordered for supper had offset any lingering effects of the alcohol. Richard leaned his head back against the seat, a hand against his eyes. "I have no idea why I do it sometimes."

"Do what?" She kept her attention on the road. The follow car had drifted back and the lead car was only two ahead of her. Tiredness weighed on her. She should have had a cup of coffee, but bar coffee was only slightly above military grade industrial solvent. *Soft living and wealthy clients are spoiling me.*

"Keep up with Armand when he decides he's in a good mood." Richard's rueful words held a trace of a slur. "I should have stopped at the first glass of wine instead of finishing the bottle with him." He patted her thigh lightly. "You were the smart one, paying attention and switching to water so you could be sober to drive, but I suppose you had to be. You drive everywhere, even when you let me drive." His laugh came out a little hollow and Kate considered how many glasses of wine he'd drunk.

She'd counted three and a half—enough to share one bottle. The second could have happened when she had to excuse herself for the restroom. If they'd traded out bottles, she might have missed it. "Did you take your medication at six?"

He'd eaten sparingly—he and the prince had begun a debate on French politics and the elections approaching in the U.K.

"You watched me do it." He walked his fingers against her leg, back and forth, as though fascinated by the fabric.

Waiting until after she'd gotten on the highway heading toward his house along the coast, she tapped his fingers lightly to get him to move.

"Sorry," Richard mumbled, but he didn't sound apologetic. Stretching an arm behind her, Kate flipped open the cooler in the well behind the driver's seat and took out a bottle of water.

"Drink," she told him sternly. It was mineral water she kept in the car for post workouts and when she was feeling rundown. It did have some caffeine in it, but not enough to upset his current restrictions and better to flout that one than the alcohol.

"Bossy." He grinned. "I like bossy. You like being the bossy of me."

Her lips twitched in spite of herself and she cut a sideways glance at him. Instead of drinking, he stared at her. It was hard to make out his features in the low light when she had to keep the majority of her attention on the road. "You pay me to be the boss of you."

"No, I pay you to be my assistant. Miranda made assistant mean the boss of my schedule."

"You live by your schedule," she countered. "Drink."

He opened the bottle and took a long swallow

obediently. "I do live by my schedule. Lots of things to keep track of." Traffic leaving the city thinned and the follow car was only one behind them.

"You could pare your schedule down." After the last few weeks, she'd seen plenty of cases he could hand off to junior associates in his firm. Cases like the Johnson one—he didn't need to hand hold so many cases personally or put in so many billable hours above and beyond the work he did for the grand duke, his extended family and the multi-billion-dollar corporations they operated.

"If I fired Armand as a client, he would be pretty pissed." Richard laughed. "And I like working with him."

"You have other clients." Like the files he kept in his locked drawer. Cases he worked on that she knew nothing about.

Richard sighed. "That's good work and I won't give them up. I had to let too many go to others while I was recuperating."

Curiosity swiped at her. "Do you mind if I ask you a question?"

He shifted in his seat, turning his head so he just stared at her. "I'm near to sloppy drunk in your car and I think I was trying to feel you up a minute ago. That definitely earns a question."

Another smile tugged her mouth wide. He made an adorable drunk, a lot like he'd made an adorable pit bull about the actor on the golf course. The quiet fury in his eyes had stunned her. She was more than capable of taking care of herself and the little nuisance was easily ignored, still—he'd wanted to defend her and that counted a lot in her books. "Why do you take all those pro bono cases? I get giving back, but you're on at least a dozen different non-profit boards that have nothing to do with the Dagmar Foundation in addition to the work you do for the Foundation. You write checks monthly to several inner-city organizations and the LAPD fund for fallen officers." Pressing him for more information in his current state didn't seem ethical, but she was curious. "What are you trying to make up for?"

He went quiet for so long, she thought he might have fallen asleep. It might be for the best, considering the dangerous line between professional and personal she teetered on. The information focused on him, the man, instead of him, the protectee. Yet, she wanted to know. He was a bit of a marvelous find, generous to a fault, and in possession of a work ethic that didn't quit.

And angry? Angry he went from handsome good boy to sexy bad boy.

"When I was seven years old, the FBI came to my door and arrested my father. My sister Barbara was four, she didn't understand what was going on. My mother was in the kitchen, the doorbell rang and these men in black suits poured inside. They had a warrant, so they took my father into custody and then went through our house. My sister and I had to sit on the floor in the living room while my mother answered questions she really didn't want to answer." His words didn't slur, but his tone managed to sound faraway. "What I didn't understand was what my father had done wrong. After they tore up our house, they took a lot of boxes with them. A week later, my dad still wasn't home and a notice was served on the house—a legal seize order."

Kate frowned, because while the man sitting next to her was strong, capable and fierce—he'd been seven years old. What an impossible situation for a child.

"You see, my father had gotten involved in a scheme with a couple of other men. They thought it would help them make some money. At first it was a few hundred here and a few hundred there. Nothing big, but one of the men took it larger and he'd bilked some retirees out of about two hundred and fifty thousand dollars. My father—knowingly or not—helped him do it and he profited by it. They froze his bank accounts, took the house—took everything—and we had to live in a woman's shelter downtown for ten weeks."

"Christine's Center." She knew the name. That name had been on one of the folders he'd locked away, but he also represented the center in several legal matters and the documentation she'd dropped off earlier had also been related to the center.

"Yes. Mom got a job pretty much right away and started saving, but we stayed there free and, during the day, the staff looked after Barbara and me. Eventually Mom had enough to move us into a tidy little apartment and things seemed to go back to normal. Dad came home when I was eight." Another long silence. They'd reached the exit and traveled up on the long winding road to his house. Fortunately, she had his address programmed into her GPS and she'd been there before during daylight hours. "He moved back in, went back to work, and it all seemed like something out of a bad dream. We got a new house. Barb and I got a new school...normal. We'd gone back to normal."

Her stomach clenched.

"But another year goes by and the men are back at our door. Same story, only this time, Dad went to jail for five years. Mom lost her job and no one would hire her because it was all over the papers. I was old enough to understand that my father screwed a lot more people out of their money—retirees, single moms, families—and he hid the money this time. So when they came and took everything from us, they still couldn't find the money, but neither could my mom." Anger, old and sullen, crept into his voice. "So we were back at Christine's Center and Mom had to take every menial job she could get her hands on. We got lucky. One of the center's benefactors thought enough of Mom to hire her, then sent her to school to get a degree. When Dad got out that time, she didn't take him back."

She pulled up to the gate and opened the window to type in the code. The external floodlights had come on upon their arrival and his expression was so dark and sad, her heart twisted.

"Anyway." Richard exhaled, sobering. "Places like that? They saved our lives twice. The people I help, those cases, they're usually getting screwed by someone like my father."

Pulling up and following the circular drive to stop in front of his house, Kate put the car in park. "Richard, you didn't do any of those things. You don't have to make amends for your father."

"Yes, I do, because he sure as hell never will." Clearing his throat, Richard unlocked his seat belt and looked at his house. "You shouldn't have to drive all the way back. I have a guest room and plenty of spare clothes here."

Driving back wouldn't be a problem. The gates were locked and the security watching the house was already in place, but the loneliness in his voice tugged at her. Shutting off the car, she glanced at him. "Is your sofa comfortable?"

"Probably." He had the smallest of smiles, pleased with her question. "But I'll tell you another secret."

"And that is?"

"I have a ton of extra bedrooms." He waggled his eyebrows and gave her a conspiratorial wink. "You can test every bed and pick the one that's just right."

Laughing in spite of the bad joke, she shook her head. "Do I look like Goldilocks to you?" Climbing out, she met him at the passenger door. When he swayed on his feet, she slid an arm around him and he braced his weight on her shoulder.

"Alyx is right. You deserve a raise."

"Hmm, if you remember this in the morning, I'll let you give me one." Between the two of them, they got the door open and he gave her the passcode for the alarm system. She disarmed then rearmed it again before guiding him toward the stairs. His staggering steps worried her, but she could handle the extra weight.

When he directed her toward his bedroom, she helped him inside and seated him on the bed. He gave her another lopsided grin and flopped onto his back.

"Hmm, no more alcohol for you, Mr. Prentiss." She tugged his shoes off, then pulled the cover from the end of the bed up over his suit. No way she would undress him.

His hand closed over hers on the duvet. "Kate?"

"Yes, Richard?"

A broad yawn stretched his mouth and he blinked slowly. "You should wear your hair down more often. It's much prettier down."

"I'll take that under advisement," she replied drily. "Go to sleep." But his eyes were already closed and a low snore echoed back at her. After returning to the kitchen, she found bottled water in his fridge, then hunted through the cabinets to find some aspirin and his prescriptions. Both were on a shelf near the coffee pot. Back in his room, she set the items on the nightstand and paused to loosen and remove his tie, unbuttoning the top two buttons on his dress shirt.

It wouldn't do to let him strangle himself in his sleep and fell under the protectee code. But looking after him didn't require her to brush that lock of hair off his forehead.

No, that she did for herself and, thankfully, he was sound asleep and missed her slip.

She almost wished she'd gotten to know him when she'd been working for Anna—at least then she could have indulged her interest. *And let's just cut that thought off right there.*

Protectees were beyond off limits. Especially when she had to lie to this one.

CHAPTER 5
RICHARD

The pounding inside his skull hammered Richard awake. Prone, he peeled his eyelids open with a wince. Too much sunshine glowed around the white sheer of the curtains—somehow he'd forgotten to close the blackout curtains when he'd gone to bed.

When the hell did I go to bed?

Sitting slowly, the marching band in his head turned into a drum line and his stomach lurched. Half-blinded by the brutal headache, he squinted at the nightstand. A bottle of water and aspirin sat waiting for him. He dry swallowed the pills, then drained half the water from the bottle. His mouth tasted like ass and that, he decided, was the only reason he would get up.

Shoving the blanket off, he gave his disheveled suit a baleful look. He hadn't fallen into bed fully clothed since... His aching head refused to cooperate. At least he'd made it home. With a care for the pulse thrumming from his brain to his roiling gut and back up again, he made his way to the bathroom. Stripping off his suit, he turned on the shower then paused at the sink to brush his teeth while the water heated.

Twenty minutes of scalding hot water and soap later, he began to believe he might resemble human. After shaving more from habit than desire, he toweled off, finger combed his damp hair, and checked the scars on his side. Three laparoscopic incisions had saved his life. They would fade over time, but he knew they were there. Gathering up his discarded clothes, he carried them back into the bedroom and dropped them on a stack he had to send to the cleaners and pulled out a pair of slacks from the closet.

The clock said it was after eight, which meant not only was he hungover, he was also late to get to the office. His cell phone wasn't in his pants pocket or on the nightstand plugged into the charger where he usually left it. It was probably in his suit jacket with his wallet. Hopefully, he'd dropped both downstairs. Shirtless, he headed straight to the kitchen.

He needed coffee—to hell with the rules. Then he'd call Kate and let her know he would be late. An image of his hand on Kate's thigh flickered through his brain and he frowned. The sight of a folded blanket and pillow parked on the corner of his sofa stopped him in his tracks. Coffee scented the air, combined with a hint of vanilla, spice and something distinctly feminine.

Following the scents, he pushed open the door to the kitchen and stared at his assistant leaning against the counter, a cup of coffee in hand. She wore the same shirt as the day before, although it was untucked and wrinkled as though she'd slept in it, and her narrow skirt hugged her legs. Her hair hung down, brushed to gleaming and draped over one shoulder. Like the day on the golf course, the sunlight played over the strands and seemed to glint off the white flax amidst the soft gold.

"Good morning," he managed around the jerk of surprise. He had been touching her thigh—petting it—while she drove him home. Curiosity and embarrassment made for a potent cocktail on his already overtaxed system. Another spate of memories detached from the fog in his brain. He'd also spilled his guts about his father—and he *never* talked about that son of a bitch if he could help it.

Blaming it on the wine would be a mistake, he'd overindulged because finding Kate in the bar had thrown him. He'd asked her out to the musical and had been disappointed when she declined, even more so because she'd pointed out that he had a date. A date that wasn't an actual date—Diane Fowler was a reminder to check in with the center, but since he wasn't supposed to cross the professional line to the personal, he'd let Kate off the hook.

Then she'd been at the bar.

And damned if he hadn't wanted to cross the line. So what did he do instead? He got drunk like some stupid college student.

Way to go. He congratulated himself. He'd been trying to maintain a veneer of professionalism with the woman, no matter how much she fascinated him.

"Good morning." Her smile eased the kidney punch from his morals and she pointed to the mug of coffee on the counter. "I heard you in the shower and started a fresh pot. You can get away with more than one cup today. How's the head?"

"I think I owe you an apology." Talking actually increased the thunder of his headache. He picked up the mug.

"Drink your coffee." She chuckled and the soft husky sound did more for his headache than the aspirin and shower combined. "You should probably eat too. However, I draw the line at cooking breakfast."

She closed her eyes and tilted her head back. She'd chosen to stand in the one spot the morning sun spilled in the window and she seemed to be soaking it up like a cat. Taking advantage of the moment, his gaze skated over her —from bare toes to rumpled shirt. Putting that together with the blanket and pillow on the sofa, he frowned. "You slept on the couch."

"Hmm-hmm." She nodded, but didn't open her eyes. "I wasn't going to poke around in your house after you went to sleep. Besides, the sofa was more than comfortable enough." Despite her words, she tipped her head from side to side in a motion he knew helped stretch out tired and stiff muscles. It drew his attention to the slender column of her throat and the smooth expanse of skin visible between the open three buttons of her shirt.

The innocent, tired gesture turned utterly provocative and his body hummed in response. Scowling, he glared down at his coffee. *Off limits, dumbass. She works for you.* His body didn't seem to give a damn about blurring the line between professional and personal. "Kate...?"

"Sorry." She blinked and shifted to move out of the sunbeam. "I think I'm a little bit cat. Give me a beam of sunshine and I'll sleep there all day."

Wrapping his mind around the image of her sprawled in front of him—long and lean, draped only in sunshine—sent a violent wave of heat surging through his lower body. "I have a pool," he found himself offering. Once the words were out, he didn't want to take them back. "And plenty of guest suits if you want to make yourself comfortable." In fact, the more he thought about spending down time with Kate, the more he liked the idea. "We have no meetings this morning and since you're here—and if you don't object—we could just work out of the house."

Surprise flickered in her gaze, but she didn't immediately reject the idea. "Are you proposing that we take the day off?"

Together. He managed to bite off that word before blurting it out like some idiot high school jock faced with the prospect that the girl might say yes. "A half-day at least." It sounded a lot better. "No morning meetings, remember?" Of course, he'd barely recalled his name when he woke.

"Anything for this afternoon, I can re-

95

arrange." She pursed her lips, and uncertainty skated across her expression. So composed and utterly in control most of the time, the vulnerability invited him to firm their plans. Make her choose to be here. "No one is going to die if you take a day off, Richard. You've been going full throttle for weeks."

"So have you." Decided, he drained his coffee and padded over to pour himself another cup. "I'm going to make you breakfast, we're going to eat it by the pool, and you can drowse in the sun to your heart's content. Unless you have somewhere else you need to be?" His gut said no. He wanted Kate to stay.

"No, not particularly." But hesitation hitched between the words.

"Then you'll stay." He nodded and a spike of pleasure at the idea pushed his headache back further. "The only job I need you to do today is to make sure I don't go to work."

Her brows lifted. "A day off spent with your assistant is not really a day off." When he held up the coffee pot she extended her mug and he refilled it. This close, the scent of vanilla spice he'd discovered in the living room grew stronger.

"So, I'll spend it with my friend Kate." He slid the pot back onto the burner and smiled. "I'd like to get to know my friend better." *I'd like to get her naked and see just what it takes to melt that professional demeanor so I can play with that sassy woman I keep getting glimpses of*—cutting off the thought before his cock stiffened any further, he reclaimed his mug.

"Richard..." Kate glanced down at her mug and the uncertainty turned to unease. Guilt flooded through him. "I'm not sure how good that idea would be."

"I am an excellent friend." Not that his life had room for a lot of them, Armand took up an elephant's amount of space. Getting personal with Kate was a terrible idea, they worked together—correction, she worked *for* him. Dammit, he wanted her to stay. Not wanting to get personal didn't mean they hadn't been. He knew all the cons and he didn't care. "But I'm not going to leverage our working relationship to demand anything more than a down day for both of us." If she headed out that door, then so be it.

"I didn't think you were." She looked from her coffee to him and he could feel the weight of her gaze like a caress on bare skin. Her attention was on his chest and he felt like puffing it out a bit, but smothered the urge. "It actually sounds great to just hang out and *be* for the day."

"But?" He eased a little closer, then leaned against the counter. "I heard the distinct *but* in there."

Their gazes locked and for a split-second, he read heat in her gorgeous eyes. Then her lashes dipped, hiding it before he could see anything more and her mouth twisted into a smile. "But I don't think you know how to relax."

He knew a challenge when he heard one. "Then maybe you don't know me as well as you think you do."

"Oh, I know you." She grinned. "We're keeping score, remember?"

Delighted by the play, he pushed away from the counter and pulled open the fridge. He'd promised her breakfast. "I do remember. So how about a wager?" Unfortunately, his fridge only had bottles of water, a couple of sandwiches in takeout boxes, and creamer for the coffee. He didn't remember the last time he'd stocked food —or did he? Miranda usually arranged for a grocery delivery, but she'd left weeks before and he'd eaten out or at the office since then.

"Depends, what are we wagering on exactly?"

"Well we're not wagering on breakfast because I would lose." He glanced at his bare wrist and scowled. His watch was upstairs and he hadn't tracked down his cell phone yet. "What time is it?"

"Nine," she answered. She set her coffee cup on the counter and padded out of the kitchen. He followed behind her and when she bent at the waist, reaching over the back of a chair, he fixed on her bottom—the skirt shaped it perfectly. By the time she'd turned back to him, with his jacket in hand, he'd gotten his wandering gaze back to safer territory. "You left this in the car last night."

"Thank you and thank you for driving me home." He fished into his pockets for his cell phone. He had a dozen urgent emails and a couple of messages from Armand, including one asking about a racquetball game. Answering it automatically, he postponed for a couple of days, then scanned his emails.

"And that's one point to me. Too bad we didn't actually decide on the bet." Her amusement curved around him like a teasing brush of her fingertips. Kate sat perched on the arm of the sofa, one golden leg crossed over the other. All sleek muscle, the woman had nothing spare on her. Her grin widened. "You're in your email. That's not taking the day off. So point to me."

He grimaced and tabbed out of his inbox. "Habit. I wanted to call and get some food delivered, or we're going to starve. There's a great little bakery up the road, how about we break all the rules and get high on sugar while we play?"

"That's definitely living on the edge." Her lips twitched.

Amused by her mocking, he pointed a finger at her. "Go find yourself something comfortable to wear in the changing room. It's right through there." He pointed down a hall. "I'll get the food ordered and meet you at the pool. Our day off starts right now."

She straightened and saluted him crisply. "You should probably change too. The slacks and the pool won't mix." Pivoting on her heel, she headed in the direction he indicated and he glanced down.

He'd been talking to her shirtless the entire time. Nothing said sexy like pale skin and scars.

Screw it. She's about to see me in swimming trunks and I get to see her in a bathing suit.

It was his day off and he wanted to flex the rules a little. He put in an order for the food delivery and paid for it with his credit card.

Glancing at the pillow that still held the barest impression of where her head had rested the night before, guilt stabbed him. He'd have to give her a tour of the house so she'd feel comfortable with a bed the next time she stayed over. Yes, there would be a next time. He was enough of a realist to recognize his interest.

It took him ten minutes to return to his room, change into swim trunks and return. Retrieving their coffee cups from the kitchen and some bottles of water, he headed out to his pool. He'd have to make it clear to her that the only reason he carried his phone as well was so he'd be alerted when breakfast was delivered.

The tiered patio and swimmer's paradise pool were two of the reasons he'd bought his house. Perched comfortably on a hill overlooking the ocean, he also enjoyed a spectacular view and privacy from even his closest neighbor a half-mile down the beach. No one out front could see his little haven and no one on the beach below would see him unless he stood next to the railing.

Kate was at the opposite end of the pool, a deep green one-piece bathing suit hugging every curve. He forgot to think when she executed a clean dive into the water. Her long arms flexed with each slice as she swam from the deep end toward him. The moment she touched the wall, she arced away, perfectly graceful to swim back the way she'd come.

Sinking onto a chair, he set the mugs, phone and water bottles on the table and just watched her swim. Back and forth, she performed the laps like a professional—he could see where she'd gotten her trim physique. By the time she completed ten laps and came up for air, he had most of his hormones under a tight leash.

"All right." She drifted over to rest against the side of the pool and grin at him. "This is definitely a perk."

"The pool?" It delighted him that she liked it.

"The pool. The day. It's beautiful." The sun glinted off the water droplets sliding down the curve of her cheek.

Yes, she was. "It's why I bought the place." He braced his feet against the warm concrete and let the heat soak in against his back. The coffee and the company had done wonders for his hangover.

"You like swimming?" She leaned back into the water and slicked her hair away from her face.

"I do, but it was for days like this. Days when I could just be out here and be alone, not worry about someone staring at me or watching for me to do something or make a mistake." It sounded very Dickensian. "That came out wrong."

"You like your privacy." She flexed her arms, then pulled herself out of the water to sit on the side, feet dangling. "I get it."

A long thin, pink line bisected her left shoulder blade and disappeared behind the razorback of the suit. Rising, he walked over and crouched next to her. Tracing the scar, he frowned. "What happened here?" Her muscles went rigid under his touch and he hesitated, curling his fingers toward his palm. "Sorry," he murmured.

"Just surprised me, is all." She shook her head and her shoulders relaxed a fraction. "And that?" She twisted to glance at her shoulder and laughed. "Oh, I'd almost forgotten I had that."

Shifting to sit next to her, he dropped his feet into the water and braced his palms on the pool edge—that should help him keep his hands to himself. "I sense a story there."

"Not a very exciting one. Actually, it's a pretty stupid story, now that I think about it." The combination of her self-deprecating tone and rueful expression elicited an altogether tender response that he didn't want to examine too closely.

"Now you have to tell me." He nudged her shoulder with his. "You got my deep, dark secret out of me last night." He never talked about his father, the subject guaranteed to put him in a black mood, but in this moment, sitting in the sunshine next to Kate, the shadow passed by with nothing more than a twist to his heart.

"To be fair, you need to understand that I grew up on an army base with three older brothers and their four best friends. These hooligans got into everything." She made a face and he grinned. He really didn't know much about the woman behind the efficient assistant beyond her sharp intelligence and occasionally saucy bites of wit. "As the youngest and a girl—" she grimaced, "—I was often excluded from some of their more exciting adventures."

"And that didn't sit well with you." An educated guess, but he knew he was right.

"Hell no, it didn't sit well with me. I could do anything they could do." All feminine outrage, then she grinned. "But they were older and had a lot more freedom. They used to do this thing called creek dogging."

"Never heard of it." He slid off the side and into the water, the cooler temperature bracing against his sun-heated skin. During his convalescence, he hadn't gotten to spend much of time in the water—or in the sun, for that matter. He hadn't realized how much he'd missed both.

"Basically, you run wild in a creek area—climbing trees, going over the sides of bridges, whacking snakes and pretending it's the wilderness. Risking your damn fool neck." Damn that sounded fun. When was the last time he did something just for the fun of it? His expression must have revealed something, because she raised her eyebrows at him and laughed. "You'd probably have liked it. It was always about dares. One would dare another to do something crazy and they'd escalate. Anyway, there's this one bridge, about twenty feet up from the water? The water is also deeper there because it was where two creeks met and created a little rapid effect. The guys hooked a rope up on one side and used it to swing back and forth and then decided they'd see who could leap the farthest from the bridge and into the water."

He nodded, watching the way the memories played across her face. When she talked about the boys, she relaxed, and her tone softened with affection. She adored her brothers, but he also saw a trace of wistful sadness when she looked out over the pool as though the memories were bittersweet.

Kate cleared her throat and refocused on him. "I'd followed them, tagging along and generally being a pain in the ass. Kevin—he was seventeen at the time—was also my eldest brother. He told them all to knock it off, and he didn't really want me there, which meant it was twice as fun for me to be. The other guys didn't listen to him and over the edge they went." Her tongue skated across her lower lip and she shook her head. "Kevin is standing there telling me no way in hell was I to follow and I ran at that rail and jumped —just like they did—only my legs weren't quite long enough and my foot hit that top rail. Instead of going over legs first, I went head first."

Richard winced. "Oh shit."

"Oh shit, yeah." Her humor grew with the recollection if that was possible. "I heard the guys yell and then I hit the water. You know creeks aren't known for being really deep, or really clean, or even really empty—between the force of the fall and my angle, I went all the way down and slammed my shoulder into something. It hurt *bad* and by the time I sputtered back up, I had two brothers trying to drag me out of the water. Then we saw the blood. I'd lacerated the shoulder on a broken bottle or something, but that part didn't hurt."

He found that hard to believe. "No?"

"Nope." She grinned. "It was the dislocation that hurt."

"Ouch." He'd dislocated his shoulder during a touch football game on the quad after colliding with one of Armand's bodyguards. Damn thing had hurt for months, even after quick medical care. "But if the water was that dirty, you could have had an infection."

"I could have had necrotizing fasciitis and I wouldn't have cared. I was so damn proud of myself for having done it, for making the jump. The bleeding and the pain couldn't diminish that. 'Course my dad's and mom's reactions were less enthusiastic." Her eyes brightened and she shrugged. "I was grounded for a month and so were the boys, but do you know the best thing that happened that day?"

"What?" The light in her eyes, the window of insight into the reckless freedom of her youth, held him hostage.

"My brothers didn't make me stay behind again because I wasn't a baby and I didn't cry. So after I was all healed up, when they went creek dogging, so did I." Pride shimmered in her tone. "I got damn good at it, too, and I never missed another leap."

"I think I like your brothers. What are they doing now?" Wrong question. The light in her eyes dulled and her smile faded. Touching a hand to her knee, he frowned. "Hey, I didn't mean to bring up a bad memory."

"It's fine, just it's easier to forget some days than it is others. Kevin died about ten years ago.

Parker went down a couple of years later, a training accident." She cleared her throat. "But Beany Baby is in Germany."

"Hell, Kate. I'm sorry." He tightened his grip on her knee. Losing not one, but two brothers—that went beyond suck. It would carve out a piece of his soul if Armand died. Barb was his baby sister, and he loved her, but Armand was his family too.

"It's okay." She covered his hand with hers and gave him a tremulous smile that almost reached her eyes. "Really. They died doing what they loved and they wouldn't have wanted it any other way. They were tough guys and I haven't thought about creek dogging in years. Thank you for that."

The conversation quieted for a moment and he longed for a way to bring back the sparkle and chase away the shadow of sadness. "Beany Baby?"

She stroked her thumb in a slow circle against the back of his hand and her laughter caught him off guard. "Benjamin. I couldn't say Ben when was I was little and used to call him Bean. He was one of those kids that shot straight up—all arms and legs and no body—and Kevin and Parker called him String Bean. Well, one day when he was razzing me, I called him Beany Baby and, to his horror, that name stuck."

Loving the humor dancing in the words, he grinned. "Duly noted." Before he could add anything else, his cell phone rang and she pulled her hand away. "That," he sighed with a hint of regret. "Is probably the food." Levering himself out of the water, he went to claim the phone.

He could have wished for a few more minutes before the interruption, but they had all day. The brief glimpse into her past wasn't enough.

The more he learned about Kate, the more drawn to her he was.

But she didn't offer him another chance. By the time they'd eaten breakfast, stored away the food and returned to the pool deck, her professional reserve returned. Oh, she laughed and she teased him, but she didn't talk about her family or her life beyond a few cryptic comments that told him he'd barely scratched the surface of this complicated woman.

And he wanted...*more*.

CHAPTER 6
KATE

I t turned out to be an idyllic day and, despite reciting every reason in the book she should have gotten her ass out of there, she'd stayed. Twice more Richard's phone rang, but she gave him credit—he checked who called and let both go to voicemail. The only messages he returned were texts from the grand duke.

His best friend—can't really fault him for that one.

He'd been damn attractive when he'd walked into the kitchen, damp hair disheveled and bare chest revealing a raw, primal physique. In his dress slacks, he'd been a study in contrasts—and very, very male. Ten laps in the pool didn't do a damn thing for easing the far from professional interest her body was developing and when he traced his finger down her shoulder blade, every nerve ending in her body had fired.

Some lines weren't meant to be crossed and she'd sliced right through them, telling him about her brothers and a half-forgotten, but thoroughly thrilling, childhood memory. Leaning her hands against the counter in the bathroom she'd borrowed to take a shower and clean up from their afternoon of leisure in the sun, Kate eyed her reflection.

It had taken a lot to distance herself, but she needed to maintain those lines. Her job was to protect him—not to explore the hard, very able body she'd discovered under his ten-thousand-dollar suits. Unfortunately, her hormones remained in violent disagreement with her ethics.

A light knock at the door sent a shiver of anticipation up her spine. She wore a towel and nothing else. The only thing between her and Richard was couple of inches of door. How easy would it be to open the barrier and make this a truly unforgettable day off...

Seriously, get a grip. She cleared her throat. "Yes?"

"Sorry, Armand called. He's invited us to dinner at the tower with him and Anna and won't take no for an answer."

"Us?" She frowned. The grand duke knew damn good and well what her job was. Maybe that was why he'd included her in the invitation, but it didn't make her presence any more appropriate. Bad enough Richard had caught her in that bar the night before with the grand duke. So far, he hadn't asked her why she'd been in the complete opposite direction of where she'd dropped off the court papers or what she and the grand duke had been discussing.

A rasp of fabric against the wall told her

Richard leaned next to the door. "Yes, *us*. Armand said he enjoyed chatting with you last night and that I should bring you along."

"I don't really have anything to wear." She'd planned to put her sleep-rumpled clothes back on and head home.

Unfortunately, Richard wasn't dissuaded. "Check the closet, I'm sure you can find something in your size in there."

She'd never have credited the grand duke for being cruel. Including her in a social event in the tower—one of the most highly secured locations in Los Angeles—didn't sit well with her. *Unless...* Pulling the door open, she gave Richard an assessing look. "You're about to lose your wager, aren't you?"

He straightened immediately, but his attention dropped to her towel. "I am?"

Refusing to be sidetracked because she'd forgotten about the towel, she fisted the ends together above her breasts. "Eyes up."

Obediently, he snapped his gaze to hers. "Sorry, your towel distracted me."

"They're bad like that," she replied drily. "He invited *us* because this isn't just a social visit."

"Probably not, no." He nodded and his gaze drifted lower again. He'd showered and changed. Dressed in a navy blue T-shirt that did nothing to disguise the cut of the muscles beneath and jeans, he looked more dangerous and delicious than he did in a suit.

"I said eyes up." She could have closed the door. A part of her mind acknowledged that fact, and that she could have tabled the discussion for when she was dressed, but a rebellious streak stiffened her resolve.

"I'm trying." He grinned. "I promise."

"Hmm, so—since you lost the wager, what do I get?" The corner of her mouth twitched with pure feminine thrill at how aware of her he behaved.

"Not much, I'm afraid." His grin turned wicked in its delight. "We never did negotiate the terms."

"Verbal agreements are still binding." Her competitive spirit surged, refusing to be disappointed.

"True." He tapped a finger to his lips. "And we did agree we should wager." Leaning forward, one hand braced against the doorframe, he met her gaze evenly. "What do you want?"

The earthy, clean scent of him wrapped around her and she looked at his mouth, then back up again. Interest gleamed in his eyes and the pupils dilated with the promise of arousal. *Oh, this is bad, Kate. Throttle it back, throttle it back.* Withdrawing a step before she gave into temptation, she pasted on a smile. "I'll let you know."

Closing the door took every ounce of her self-control. She leaned back against the cool wood. For a long second, she'd imagined asking him for a kiss or just saying to hell with it and kissing him herself.

How was she supposed to protect him if she was fantasizing about getting him naked?

"Kate?" Dammit, even the way he said her

name sent another shiver to race over her skin and her nipples tightened into nearly painful points beneath the towel.

Professional, soldier. Keep it professional. "Yes, Richard?" Although husky, she managed to keep her tone level.

"Open the door."

Closing her eyes, Kate shook her head. "I'll be out in a moment. I need to get dressed."

A soft sound, a faint scrape, as though he ran his finger across the wood separating them. It teased her senses—imagining it was her skin he traced, as he had the scar on her shoulder. "I promised myself I would behave," he murmured and she had to strain to hear him. "You work for me."

"I know." *God help me, do I know.*

"But I'm thinking that you might be interested too. No harm, no foul, Kate. If you want to open the door, that's between you and me. Not the office, not the job."

Dammit. She wanted to open the damn door. But they had a lot more standing between them than the office or the job. With regret she knew would sting, she turned to flatten her palm against the wood. "I'll be down after I change."

The protracted silence that met her statement wrenched at her heart. She almost opened the door to make sure he was all right. But, then, he tapped the wood once. "Okay." The word rode a long breath, but no matter how light he made his tone, she couldn't forget the seductive rasp of his invitation. "I'll be waiting. On the up side, we got most of the day off."

"Yeah." She tried to inject some enthusiasm in her tone to disguise her struggle. "And I had fun."

"Me too, Kate. Me too." The hint of a step and he walked away. Kate stayed at the door, waiting until the last of his steps faded away before she made herself move. Personal investment in a protectee was permissible to a point. She couldn't protect someone and not care about them, because their safety was what they paid her to care about.

But she cared a hell of a lot more for Richard than professional interest allowed. She'd talk to the grand duke and— No, he was also Richard's best friend and between the two of them, they'd already lied to Richard enough. She'd talk to Peterson. He would understand the need for a replacement.

It was the right decision—the rational, calm and professional one.

So why did her stomach knot up at the idea?

By the time she'd dried her hair and come out into the borrowed bedroom, the door to the hallway was closed and she was alone. Opening the closet, she stared at the wide variety of clothes filling the space. Everything from casual to semi-formal, in different colors and—she shifted through the different hangers—different sizes.

Most were women's clothing, but some were for children. The man had a huge house and a sister, but she didn't think he had any nieces or nephews. So why all the clothes? Did he have lovers over so frequently in need of a change in clothing?

None of your business, Kate. A snarky inner voice chastised her.

Hell, many of the clothes still had the tags on them. Maybe he kept them for his sister or maybe he had a new lover every week, it didn't matter. They were clothes. She needed to pick something and put it on. At least the presence of the price tags meant she wasn't putting on some other woman's clothes.

Remembering his outfit, she chose a pair of jeans—they were just long enough to fit her legs. Forgoing a T-shirt, she chose a sleeveless button down blouse and found a blazer in the back.

She might be able to get away with moderately casual, but she still needed business dress and—frankly—the less skin she showed around Richard might be for the better.

When she walked down the stairs, her disheveled clothing over her arm, she found Richard waiting. He wore a blazer similar to the one she'd picked out, his hands tucked into his pockets. "You found something that fits. Great." And no comment about his offer on the other side of the bathroom door.

Relieved, and a little disappointed, she took

her cue from him. "I had a great selection to choose from."

"That's the idea." He nodded. "You ready to go?"

"Absolutely." Fortunately, she'd worn low-heeled pumps with her suit the day before and they worked fine with this outfit. She could run in them—something she did periodically just to say trained in the event that she'd need to. "Do you want me to drive? I can take you back by the office afterward, pick up your car." Security would have kept their eye on the vehicle that he'd left parked in the garage of the building housing his law office.

For the barest flicker of breath, frustration appeared in his eyes, but he nodded and the moment evaporated. "That would be great." He picked up his keys from the dish by the door where she'd left them and keyed in the code to disarm his security system. She went out ahead of him and scanned the area. Her SUV sat where she'd left in the circular drive. The follow car wasn't in evidence, but if she could see his security, they wouldn't be doing their job.

The little bubble of freedom encapsulating their day shrank the closer they got to the city. Conversation seemed strained and more than a little stilted. Richard's attention was fixed on the passing landscape, but then he could also be thinking about the grand duke's summons. Wherever his mind was, it wasn't on her. They were better off ignoring each other.

She believed that, so why did it still bother her that he remained so silent?

"Hey." He shifted in his seat about a block from the tower. "Stop over there—"

Already slowing and moving over to grab the street-side spot he'd indicated, she scanned the area. Steady foot traffic filled the sidewalks, people hurrying to and from the shops and likely the mall around the corner after work. A coffee shop, a newsstand and a flower kiosk also lined up along the street. "What's up?"

"I want to get some flowers for Anna." He pulled his wallet out of the inner pocket of his jacket and checked the bills inside. "She hasn't totally forgiven me for knowing about Armand before she did and, you know, it's the little things that go a long way."

"I don't think she's that angry at you." Kate saw the follow car swing past. There was nowhere for it to park near them. Protocol would have it do a pass and go around the block. *Crap.* "I'll come along."

"It's fine." Richard swung the car door open. "I'll just be a minute."

She couldn't let him go on his own.

Turning off the engine, she slid out of the car and tried to assess the number of ways this was bad and there were too damn many of them. Jogging around the hood of the car, she caught up to him before he'd made it more than a half dozen steps.

"Maybe I should get them flowers too. You

know, since they invited me to dinner." *Lamest excuse ever. Did you leave your professional brain behind?*

Richard chuckled and it was the first sound of warmth and amusement she'd heard since turning down his request to open the door. "Get Armand some pansies. He'll really appreciate that."

She had to bite her lip to keep from laughing out loud. "I don't think insulting your best friend and premier client is the way to win friends and influence people."

"I don't know..." Richard paused at one corner of the flower kiosk and began to inspect the different arrangements. "I think it would influence me greatly."

And just like that she was tempted to buy the pansies so she could enjoy Richard's reaction. Angling so she stood just behind him and to the side, she scanned the street. Tall buildings hemmed them in and crowds of pedestrians straggled past—and that didn't take into account the cars on the street.

The follow car made a pass and she made sure not to look at it. The less attention she drew to it, the better.

"What do you think of these?" Richard held out a colorful bouquet of carnations and lilies with a spray of baby's breath interweaved through them. "Do they say I'm a nice guy you want to like?"

Sparing the flowers a brief glance, she

shrugged. "They say you're a sweet, thoughtful man trying to make amends."

"So, I should add chocolate?" He studied the flowers, then the other items on the display.

"No, no chocolate." She pivoted, her attention on her car.

Just two normal people out to pick up some flowers on the way to dinner. Nothing to see here, folks.

"Women like chocolate," he argued.

"That's gender profiling and not wholly accurate. For example, *I* don't like chocolate." A man leaned against the wall across the street, but from the wear of his jeans and the dirty state of his shirt, she identified desperation and sadness, not threat.

"You don't?" Richard swung all the way around and she met his gaze.

"Not particularly, no. It's nice enough as an accent, but I'm just not a fan." Yes, she was aware it made her a bit odd, but she'd always preferred other flavors to chocolate. The world, however, disagreed, and everything swam in chocolate these days.

"What *do* you like?" He held a second bouquet, similar to the first, but boasting three white roses in the center, next to the first.

"Strawberry." She grinned. "Fruit flavors, I'm crazy about them. Most fruits I like." All the hair on her body stood up. She'd missed something. Every sense went into high alert.

"Interesting. Do you think this is better with or without the roses?"

"White roses symbolize pure love and I'm pretty sure that's not the message you're planning on sending." What had she missed? Her gut clenched.

The follow car went around again. The kid across the street was still there. A homeless person sat parked in the breezeway between two buildings. The world slowed down. A group of teens were arguing loudly about their evening plans. The coffee stand did a brisk business for five-thirty in the afternoon.

"So yellow, then. Those are friendship."

"Yes, white is pure, yellow is friendship, and red is lust." Her palms itched. He needed to pick out his flowers and they needed to get back in the car. "Find the ones you want?"

"Almost." He circled around the kiosk and stood on the building side of it. "Why not chocolate?"

"What?" She started to follow, but a glimmer caught the corner of her eye. The world slowed down as she traced the movement—*where had she seen it?* A car parked illegally on the other side of the street and the driver's side door opened. Sun gleamed off the windows above and cast a glare that bounced off the passing vehicles.

"These are perfect. All carnations, lots of different colors, with lilies and something else I have no idea what it is, but it's pink—so maybe she'll like it. Why not chocolate?" Richard stopped right next to her, but she wasn't focused on him. All she saw was the gun.

Turning hard, she drove her shoulder and hip into his much larger frame. They went down in a tangle of arms and legs as three hard, hollow cracks echoed over the street traffic.

And that's when the screaming started.

RICHARD

His heart stopped and he forgot to breathe. When Kate had stumbled and collided with him, he'd started to catch her, but then they both hit the pavement. The sound of the bullets, the flower baskets around them, and the shop window behind them exploded the air. Water and glass rained over them and Richard wrapped a hand around Kate's head and tried to shield her.

People screamed, tires squealed and then another set of tires squealed. In the distance sirens cut over the din. Richard shifted. "Kate?" When she didn't answer immediately, ice slithered through his veins and he sat, carrying her with him. "Kate?"

She swung wide eyes to look at him. Her disheveled hair spilled around her face and the shoulder of her jacket was soaked with water. "Are you hurt?"

Men in dark suits swarmed onto the sidewalk and Richard recognized them as Armand's security force. He'd thought as much when he'd noticed the same car following them on their way into town. When he'd made Kate pull over to get flowers, it had been so he could confirm it.

"Mr. Prentiss?"

"Ms Braddock?" Five of them in all—though Richard had only seen two in the car. This close to the tower, the others had probably come down to see what the holdup was.

"I'm fine." Tabling his rage for the time being, Richard ran his hands up and down Kate's arms. "Are you hurt?"

"We should get off the street." She glanced at the men surrounding them and her composure seemed to be waging a comeback. One of the men caught her arm and helped her up. Richard accepted the hand of another guard and then tugged her away from the suits. Water trickled across his hand. He glanced down.

It was red.

"Kate?" His gaze went to her wet shoulder.

"I'm fine, we need to go." Cool, collected and offering him direction. "Someone was shooting."

"We can handle the police." One of the suits stepped forward, but Richard ignored all of them and pushed her blazer off her shoulder. It wasn't soaked with water at all.

Blood trickled down her arm.

A man closed the gap and between them. They got the blazer off and he held out a cloth to put pressure over the wound.

"It's a scratch." Cool as cucumber, Kate's mouth tightened at the pressure.

"We need a hospital." He looked at Armand's team. One thing he could count on them for— they would make it happen. They complied, hustling them both into the backseat of an SUV.

"Richard—" She started to cut him off.

"Shut up." He wasn't playing and he wrapped an arm around her waist and tugged her closer so he could keep up the pressure on her arm. "You're going to the hospital. Understood?"

Her eyebrows rose, but she nodded once. "Understood."

Heart hammering, adrenaline raced through him. He should have just confronted Armand at dinner rather than trying to make a point. If he hadn't made Kate pull over, if he hadn't tried to prove the men were following him—fury poured through him.

"I'm okay, Richard," Kate murmured in a very soft voice and he knew it was for his benefit—the others were focused on the road.

"Shut up," he repeated the words, but softened his harsh tone. He tucked her closer. She'd gotten shot at because she was with him. She was *hurt*.

An hour later he stood in the waiting area, hands in his pockets, and staring hard at the wall. Two of the men in suits had stayed with him after he'd ordered a third one to stay with Kate. The doctors had taken her down for an x-ray despite her continued insistence that she was fine. When more dark suits filtered into the waiting area around him, he knew Armand had arrived.

"How is she?" It was a testament to their

friendship that Armand asked about his assistant first.

"The bullet didn't penetrate anything vital as far as they could tell, but they took her for x-rays." It took effort to keep his tone calm when all he wanted to do was punch something.

"Good. How are you?" Concern echoed in the question.

"Trying to decide if I want to kick your ass or shake your hand and say thank you." He read the other man's face clearly. Armand wasn't remotely sorry about the security despite Richard ordering him to take the detail off him. "I stopped because I spotted your guys."

"Then they didn't do their jobs well." There was no apology in his voice. "Because you were shot at."

"It could have been a drive by. Those happen in L.A." A sad fact of urban life—not everything was a damn conspiracy.

"Except it was a single shooter. Reports said the man pulled over, got out of his car and opened fire. Descriptions vary. The police will want to talk to you and Kate to see if they can get a more accurate description."

The problem was Richard hadn't seen any-thing. He'd been too busy looking at Kate. She'd turned him down at the house and he'd agreed to respect that decision. It was the smart thing to do and then someone shot at him—at her. "Why the continued detail? I thought I told you I didn't want them around anymore."

"No, you said you were tired of them being

under foot. So I had them pull back." A warning note echoed in Armand's voice. "A decision I am currently rethinking."

"No." Richard shook his head. "I don't need babysitters and I don't need an armed force walking me in and out of the places I have to go." Despite no one being close enough to listen, he kept his voice low, then bit off the next words on the edge of his tongue. They weren't friendly and Armand didn't deserve the biting edge of his temper—even if his best friend *had* overstepped. An armed cadre of men might look safety to some, but they'd do nothing but terrify others.

"I understood that, and I respected it." Armand shook his head. "What if the next bullet isn't astray? Do you expect me to sit by and do nothing while my enemies target you?"

"That's a little melodramatic." Turning away, Richard glanced down the hall. No sign of the doctors, or of Kate. He wanted to know she was all right, to just touch her one more time to be sure. "She didn't cry."

"What?"

"She didn't cry," he repeated. The fist clenching inside his gut hadn't eased since he'd seen the blood trickling over his hand. She didn't make a sound or a whimper—just one swift indrawn breath when they'd begun to apply pressure to her shoulder. Sitting poolside, she'd told him the story about the scar on her shoulder and how she didn't cry when she'd dislocated and cut it during her fall. *I wasn't a baby,* she'd laughed, *and I didn't cry.*

Tough, beautiful, composed—she didn't have to be. But she hadn't cried when he'd been upset and furious. Instead, she'd told him over and over she was okay, despite the fact that he snapped at her.

"Richard, I don't want to scale back your security. This is two attempts in a few months and the first time you were out in a public location. The person who ran you off the road was never apprehended." As modulated as Armand's tone was, as reasonable as he attempted to sound, the note of fear underscoring it all remained. His best friend was worried about him.

Richard was worried about Kate.

She went everywhere with him.

"Fine, keep your guys on me, but I still want them at a distance and I want a detail on Kate too."

"Done."

Curious at the easy agreement on the second part, Richard turned back to study him, but one of the security men allowing a nurse into the waiting room grabbed his attention. "Mr. Prentiss?"

He forgot about Armand. "How is she?"

"Ms Braddock is fine. She's back in the exam room if you want to come and see her."

He absolutely did. "I'm going to have to take a rain check for tonight. I'll call you tomorrow."

"I can wait," Armand offered, but Richard shook his head.

"I'll stay here with her or get her home—I don't suppose one of these guys can get her car?" Unless it was part of the active crime scene.

"Already done." His friend assured him.

"Thank you—oh, and don't think this lets you off the hook. I'm still pretty pissed." But the statement lacked any real heat and the prince didn't look remotely worried.

"As long as you're alive to be angry, I'm fine with that." And no doubt he was.

Shaking his head, Richard strode down the hall and followed the nurse. Two of his suited babysitters moved with him, but if it kept Kate safe—he could put up with his skin crawling due to the constant observation.

She was alone in the room when he entered, a white bandage bright and stark against her tanned skin. "I told you I was fine," she began as he walked in the door.

"Shut up." He pushed the door closed, leaving the security outside.

"You and I are going to have a very real problem if you keep that up." Anger snapped in her eyes and his gaze focused on her mouth.

The fist in his gut eased, but he didn't miss a beat and simply rephrased the argumentative statement. "I'm sorry, will you please be quiet?"

"No, why do you keep telling me to shut up?" Confusion threaded through her irritation and the second knot of tension in him eased.

"Because every time you start talking, I want to kiss you." His focus lingered on her mouth and, at her abrupt silence, he let it travel up to meet her gaze. "You scared the hell out of me."

Instead of answering, she licked her lips.

"Okay, what did the doctor say?"

She raised her eyebrows and he smiled, bracing one hand on either side of where she sat on the exam bed.

"You can answer. I'll do my best to restrain my urge to kiss you."

"Richard." She tilted her head and her voice took on that coaxing note, the one she used to manage him so well in the office. "I'm fine. It's a scratch. No bone damage, nothing a couple of stitches and a big Band-Aid couldn't fix."

"As soon as they discharge you, I'll take you back to my place for a couple of days. You can rest." He gave in to one urge and tucked some loose strands of her hair behind her ear.

"I don't think that would be a good idea."

"I don't care. You shouldn't be driving." He walked right over her objections. "I have a huge house, plenty of guest rooms, and an excellent security system. We can get some work done, if you insist."

"I have an apartment." She frowned at him.

"I don't care." He brushed his knuckles down her cheek. She was okay.

It might take him a little while to really believe it, though.

"Richard, it's a bad idea." And he didn't wonder what she meant.

"Do you remember what I said about no harm, no foul?" This close he could count the flecks of gold in her eyes.

"Yes. We work together and it would be inappropriate." Her nostrils flared and her gaze never left his. She was as aware of him as he was of her.

"I changed my mind." And he leaned in closer, nose barely brushing hers. He kept his actions slow and deliberate. If she wanted to push him away, he'd go. Her soft sigh brushed his cheek and he smiled—he knew capitulation when he heard it and closed the remaining distance to press his lips to hers.

He'd meant to only sample her lips, a sweet, chaste kiss—a promise for later. She'd been shot. But the electric contact lit a chemical reaction and, when her mouth parted beneath his, he deepened the kiss, seeking and gaining entry with his tongue. Her palm came into contact with his chest, but instead of pushing him away, she curled her fingers into his shirt and dragged him closer. Then her tongue dueled furiously with his.

The world fell away and lust rushed in to fill all the places heated by his anger. He gripped the bed to keep from exploring her curves. With regret, he broke the kiss slowly and was pleased to find her breathing as ragged as his own. "We have a problem," he told her, but he didn't care one whit.

"I think so." She swallowed and her gaze clashed with his. Red flushed her cheeks and her eyes were bright. "It goes against all the rules."

"You know what I've learned over the years?" He traced the slick line of her mouth with his gaze.

"What?"

"When the rules don't work, change them."

His heart jackhammered against his ribs, but he narrowed the divide between them, then whispered. "Are you willing to negotiate a rule change with me?"

She bit her lower lip and the innocence in the action stabbed at him. This self-possessed, composed, wildly competent and intelligent woman bit her lip like a girl far less sure of her confidence. Stunned by her reaction, he eased back. Her lashes swept down and then up again. "This is dangerous territory."

Understanding her reluctance and caution, he nodded. He'd shared it, and whether it was the security detail following him, the gunshots fired at them, seeing the blood trickling down her arm or some leftover unresolved remnant from his near fatal car crash a few months before, Richard didn't want to keep playing it safe.

Not anymore.

"So was creek dogging," he pointed out.

The corner of her mouth twitched. "Are you warning me that kissing you will be a lot like creek dogging?"

"Doing insanely foolish things for the thrill of it?" he replied, and kissed the sassy corner of her mouth. "Hell yes."

~

INTERESTINGLY ENOUGH, she refused to argue with him while Armand's security drove them to her apartment until they were both inside and their escort outside. "This is ridiculous." She touched the sling on her arm. "It's a scratch. I can stay here and be in the office first thing Monday morning—or even tomorrow morning."

"No." He disagreed and found it extremely easy to tell her so. Glancing around her apartment was enlightening and he fought the urge to explore. It was small, but comfortable. The two-bedroom was in a twenty story building just fifteen minutes from his office. He wanted to kick himself for how often they ended the work day more than an hour away from her apartment, yet she'd never complained. "You want me to go pack for you?"

"Richard, I don't need to come and stay at your house. It's a thoughtful offer, but I'm good. Really." She set her purse down on the white oak, Queen Anne table. The number of dings and scratches in the wood cried out it was an old family piece and likely hauled for sentimental value. It matched nothing else in the room full of muted earth tones brightened by jewel tone accents and neat, orderly simplicity. A Kindle sat on the arm of the sofa, and books were scattered on the shelves. His palms itched to go and see what types of books she liked to read. He had the ridiculous urge to know everything about her.

"You've still got the adrenaline going from the attack and probably a little bit of shock—not to mention the local anesthetic they used before they stitched you up. Tomorrow will be more uncomfortable. At my place, I can look after you, make sure you take your meds and you can sit and soak up the sun. It's a win-win." He sidled over to her and grinned. "Turnabout's fair play. You've been looking after me since your first day in the office and I know you weren't fooled about how tired I was."

"That's different," she argued. Instead of going toward her bedroom, she headed for her tiny kitchen. Despite the slender length of it, a large window filled the space with light. Popping the fridge open, she extracted a bottle of water.

Richard reached over and unscrewed the top for her. "No, it's not. The only difference is you didn't know me, you walked into a hellacious job and you didn't complain—not once—about the amount of work it took to catch me back up. In the office at seven and not out again until ten or eleven at night. I don't think you've had a day off since you started."

"But I got to watch you play golf and eviscerate a douchebag." She grinned and took a drink of her water. He'd acted purely on impulse the day he'd picked her up for that game. She hadn't needed to be there, but she'd tagged along and walked the entire course, standing in the sun and been pawed by the "actor" brother-in-law. No, he hadn't needed her there. He'd *wanted* her there.

"Yeah, that just tells me I owe you more." He blew out a breath. "Honey, you can keep fighting me on this and I'll stand here and argue with you, but I'm an attorney. I can argue all night."

"Okay, one you can't just walk into a hospital room, tell me I am staying with you for the weekend, follow me home and continue the argument.

I'm your assistant, not your girlfriend." A struggle played across her expression.

"I know, but you're my *friend* Kate. I like my *friend* and I want to take care of her. Can you let me do that?"

Their gazes clashed. He understood the difficulty—hell, he wrestled with his own issues. A part of him thought she would be better off far away from him—but the selfish part of him didn't want to send her away. Armand had him under watch, apparently whether he liked it or not, so the safer place was with him.

After all, isn't that what I told Armand when he was so determined to push Anna away for her own good?

"You don't fight fair." She set the bottle down and rested back against the counter. Her statement of the obvious suggested she wavered, but she'd hardly given up.

"I fight to win." A truth he had long since come to accept about himself. "I'm going to go pack a bag for you. What do you want?"

"I can't sleep with you Richard." Her quiet words stopped him. "We would be crossing a line we can't take back."

Leaning on the doorframe to her kitchen, he stared at her levelly. "I know. You work for me. Sleeping with me has not been, is not, and never will be a condition of that employment. But I know we're a little bit more than employer and employee—and I know you feel it too."

"It doesn't matter what I feel or don't." She

ran her tongue over her upper lip and shook her head. "It doesn't change the facts."

"It can," he said softly, because what he said in the next few minutes could very well change the direction they went. He really wanted to control the steering of that particular course. Maybe they'd only had a few weeks to get to know each other, but what he knew of her he liked and dammit—he wanted more. "We make rules, we negotiate them, and we don't break anything or change until we're both ready."

"Life is not a negotiation. Not always." Not a rejection.

"It can be, if you want it bad enough." His had been. He didn't like the life he'd grown up in—one stained by his father's dishonesty and double dealings—so he'd changed his life by changing the rules. "But this? Right now? This isn't about taking you home to my bed, stripping off your clothes and kissing you until we can't see straight. See, I know that's a potential outcome and it's an attractive one. But that's not what I'm asking you for or what I am trying to accomplish. Tonight."

Blowing out a long breath, she gave him a skeptical look. "What are you asking?"

"You. Me. My house. The weekend. Tonight through Monday morning at eight a.m. We're not an attorney and his assistant. It's not about the office or the job—just you and me. Richard and Kate. Spending a weekend together, getting to know each other and letting me look after you so I don't worry that you're okay." It sounded damn good to him. They could always renegotiate later.

"Can I get that in writing?" The smile curving her mouth teased him. "Specific terms and definitions."

"Contracts favor the one who writes them." He glanced around her kitchen and spotted a legal pad. He grabbed it and a pen, carried them over and set them next to her. A phone number was in the upper right hand corner of the pad. He recognized it instantly. Armand's private number at the tower. He paused. Then, remembered Anna, how fondly the women spoke of each other. He wouldn't be surprised if they too had formed a deeper employer/employee relationship. Though, he doubted contract terms were involved in their friendship.

Tearing off the top sheet and laying it aside, he held up the pen. "Dictate the terms."

"You're serious?" She studied him, disbelief and—*dare he hope?*—a hint of enchantment in her eyes.

"Deadly." He nodded once and waited, pen poised over the paper. "Terms, woman. Name the terms."

"Fine. The following contract and terms, to be hereinafter known as 'The Contract' will be between Kate Braddock and Richard Prentiss, hereinafter known as 'The Parties' with regard to the next—" she paused to look at the clock on her stove, "—sixty-eight hours. Expiring at zero-eight hundred, Pacific standard time, Monday."

He grinned at the "hereinafters" and the definition of "the parties." Adding Monday's date to it, he glanced up. "Someone's been paying attention."

"After the seventy-four we've written, reviewed or amended in the last four weeks, I should hope so."

"Seventy-four? Are you sure?"

"The consortium contracts—we had to write out individual ones for each negotiation and each company licensing *Spherecast* software." The amused impatience in her tone drew another grin from him.

"True. All right, point to you. Next, terms?" He tapped the legal pad.

"Impossible man," she muttered.

He wrote down *Richard must be impossible.*

"That is not a term." Her mouth formed an "o" and he had to bite his tongue to keep from kissing her.

"You said it, it goes in, and I don't have a problem with that stipulation." Hell, he rather enjoyed imagining how many ways he could be impossible.

"Fine." Straightening, she tapped the top of the legal pad. "The parties will sleep in separate bedrooms, shower in separate bathrooms. They will refrain from intimate contact, with a minimum of six—no, make that twelve—inches of distance between them at all times. Conversations may include friendly banter, but must avoid overt sexual advances and at no point will I sleep with you."

Richard grinned and read his way through

the contract. Damn if she didn't give him a lot of wiggle room, particularly with the first item. "I have no problems signing this."

"For a contract to be valid, it has to have three things." She stopped his signature with a finger on the back of his hand. "An offer, an acceptance..."

"...and consideration." The woman's mind never quit. "I think your brain is the sexiest thing I've ever known."

"That falls under sexual advances," she countered, but she was smiling. Yes, he had her. The last knot in his gut relaxed. She was brilliant, but when it came to cutthroat negotiations, he was better and he knew how to close this deal.

"The offer is my house and care for the weekend. The acceptance is you spending the weekend with me under my care." He added that to the contract.

"And the consideration?"

The sizzle in his blood turned up at the arch challenge in her voice. "I don't suppose you'd let me take it out in trade?"

"Nope." But she laughed again.

"Consideration is just quid pro quo. I want to get to know you better and this arrangement lets me do it—and it gives you a chance to get to know me."

"I do know you," she murmured, and the soft whisper of her voice stroked him. "Pretty well, I think."

"Then how about it gives you a fair opportunity to change your mind about pursuing an off hours relationship—no harm, no foul if you decide against it." He wanted her like he wanted air. Getting her to his place for the weekend, that was a win, but he played for stakes in the longer game.

"And this is fun and enticing as hell, but saying yes? That's the thing chaos is made of." She still wasn't saying *no*.

"So, all we need is consideration. That's not a yes or a no."

Retreating a step, Kate rubbed her hand against the back of her neck and he could see the exhaustion weighing on her. She ended his internal debate with another exasperated sigh. "The hell with it. Put it on there. I'm tired and you're right—you have a great pool."

Scrawling his signature, he turned the pad around and handed her the pen. "Now that wasn't so hard was it?"

"Said every spider to every fly ever, but game on, Mr. Prentiss. You have the next sixty-eight hours of my life."

And I'll make every single one count.

CHAPTER 8
KATE

Peterson waited for them at the cliff-side beach house and, to her boss's credit, he didn't say a word about the overnight bag Richard carried inside or the fact that she would be staying with her protectee for the weekend.

"If you'll give us a moment, I want to get Kate settled in a guest room." The solicitous and intoxicating need he had to take care of her could prove dangerous. The only way to truly nip it in the bud was to tell him the truth—and *that* came with another inherent set of problems.

"Actually—" she paused in the living room, "—I'm fine just sitting down for a while and I would like to hear what they have to say too." What arrangements had been made while she'd been stuck getting her shoulder stitched? What had they found out about the shooter? The car? She'd given a description to the police officers and to Peterson, but the details remained sketchy.

"You should probably get some sleep." The adorable pit bull returned full force in that statement. Richard was sweet and thoughtful and it needed to stop or he'd wrap her up in cotton and she'd never be able to do her job.

"I'm physically tired, but not mentally." Countering that base protective instinct meant appealing to the logical, if ruthless, man beneath. When she'd said she knew him well, she'd meant it. Under that warm, extremely civilized exterior lurked a merciless attorney who played to win. He knew exactly how to leverage his charm to get what he wanted. She was at his house, wasn't she? "And you'll just have to tell me everything he says anyway..."

A scowl tensed his forehead, then relaxed when she didn't look away. "All right," he relented. "Do you want something to eat? We didn't have dinner." It was after eleven and they'd spent their entire evening at the hospital, then her apartment.

Shifting her attention to Peterson as she sat on the sofa, Kate murmured, "Pizza?"

His subtle nod assured her the gate security protocols wouldn't be affected by the request.

Richard sat the bag down by the steps to the upstairs before joining her and pulling out his phone. "Pineapple?"

Surprise rippled through her and she blinked. "Yes."

"You like fruit," he reminded her. "Ham and pineapple or just pineapple?"

Torn between embarrassment because Peterson observed the interaction and delight that Richard had indeed noted what she'd said earlier, she shrugged, then winced. The shoulder didn't like the movement. "Pineapple only would be great."

Five minutes and three pizzas ordered later—Richard asked for two pineapple and one meat lovers—Peterson spread out some papers on the coffee table. She recognized the layouts for beach house, office and courthouse. Shifting forward, she tried to ignore Richard's thigh brushing against hers. It violated the twelve-inch rule, but she could hardly point that out with their audience.

Slanting a sideways look at him, she found him grinning at her. *Behaving impossibly...and he damn well knows it.* His not-so-subtle wink coiled tension in her belly. *Security first then deal with Richard in private.*

"As you can see, most of your standard locations—this house, your office, and the courthouse—are relatively easy to secure. We'd like to station a man inside the gates here," he marked a spot on the property. "He can handle any deliveries, anyone seeking admission, and unless we have a champion rock climber, no one's coming up the cliff side. However, I would recommend regular patrol intervals, particularly when you're going to be outside. We've already done security checks on your neighbors and they're all clean."

"You did this a long time before tonight." The too cool tone didn't indicate a receptive attitude. If anything, Richard's chill screamed disapproval.

"His Highness requested the security checks at regular intervals anytime you had someone new move into the neighborhood." Peterson had no problem with Richard's disapproval, and why should he? He didn't work for Richard and what His Highness requested, the grand duke received.

"Fine." Richard scratched at his jaw. "I know you have the club secure, or Armand wouldn't use it."

"That's correct. We'll need to make few alterations there. As for your office, the new security protocols fall directly in line with what we would suggest, however—" Peterson's gaze switched to her, "—Ms. Braddock's apartment building is far more difficult to secure."

Don't you do it.

Her boss ignored the look she sent him.

"She's staying here this weekend. We'll address next week when we get to it." Richard took the news well. Too well. He actually smiled for the first time since the meeting started.

Son of a bitch. I need to tell Richard. Peterson's gaze fixed on her and she could almost hear his negative response. They needed to talk, but they couldn't while Richard hovered so protectively. Yes, his protectiveness served a purpose—she could effectively be glued to his side—but at what cost?

"Very well. We're going to ask you to share your schedule with us." *As if he didn't already have it. Very smooth.* "We need at least twenty-four hours' notice of any physical location changes so we can scout them ahead of time."

"Some meetings are required last minute and I won't always have twenty-four hours to let you know about them." A muscle ticked in Richard's jaw. He really hated this and Kate's heart squeezed.

Touching a hand to his, she pulled his attention to her. "We have a list of all the centers where you do representation. We can give them that and they can clear them ahead of time for security concerns or whatever it is they're looking for."

He turned his hand over and caught hers in an easy grip. "That won't prevent things like what happened today."

"Precisely," Peterson agreed. "If you don't mind, I'd like to ask you both some questions about today's events. For example, why did you stop?"

"Richard wanted to pick out flowers for Miss Novak. We were on our way to the tower for supper at the grand duke's invitation." No way would she allow Richard to shoulder the blame. His mouth tightened and she squeezed his hand in comfort. "It was an impulse, so we pulled off and went over to check the flower stand."

"When did you become aware of the threat?" Peterson's gaze locked on hers and she heard the unasked question. *Why didn't she stop him from getting out of the car?*

"When the gun went off," Richard answered before she could. "It was pretty crowded and I was watching for your men. I'd noticed the vehicle following us a few times now." Cool anger

145

crept into his tone. "I wanted to be sure before I spoke to Armand about it, so I asked Kate to stop. She had no idea beyond the flowers."

Peterson didn't buy that as an excuse and neither did Kate. She'd screwed up letting him get out of that car and she'd seen the threat, but too late to prevent the attack. Seemingly letting it go, the security chief nodded. "What can you tell me about the shooter?"

Nowhere near as much as she wanted to be able to say. "White male. Maybe six foot. Dark baseball cap, longish hair, no facial hair." The scene replayed in her mind. The height comparison she took from the man's relative position to his vehicle. "Couldn't get a good physical build."

"You got a lot." Richard stroked his thumb along the side of her hand.

"What about the gun? The LAPD is running ballistics, but we may have to wait some time for that report."

The scene scrolled across her mind's eye. *The car.* It'd passed once. She'd noticed it on the second pass. The third time it had pulled up to a stop. The man climbed out. He wore a suit jacket —odd in counterpoint to the hat—but the sun was in her eyes.

"She's tired," Richard interrupted before she could answer. "Maybe we can finish this tomorrow."

"No, I'm fine," she assured him. "But I can't be sure of the gun. I see the barrel, I know it was a handgun. Could have been a .45? The pop sounded like a .45, no silencer."

"And how do you know what a .45 sounds like?" Richard pinned her with a look.

"I've fired one." It was the absolute truth and the answer didn't mollify him. "But I couldn't swear to it."

"That's fine. Make and model of the car?"

"Dark sedan, some kind of tinted windows because they really reflected the glare. Didn't see a license plate." Which amounted to a fat lot of nothing, but she knew every detail added to a bigger picture and when it came to securing a target, the more they knew the better off they were.

"That's fine. We're going to see if we can get some footage from the security cameras in the coffee shop. They might have had an angle." Peterson gathered up his papers. "Any plans to leave the house this weekend?"

"No," Richard answered. "We're locking it down for now. I can access most of my files digitally, so we won't need to go to the office."

"Excellent." Extracting two cards from his inner jacket pocket, Peterson handed one to Richard and held the other out to her. She had to tug her hand from Richard's to accept it. "Please put my number in your phones, if you think of anything—no matter how inconsequential, let us know. The LAPD is expediting the case for you, Mr. Prentiss. As you're aware, they are very fond of you."

He nodded and rose, shaking Peterson's hand once. "I'll walk you out." The two men left.

Kate flipped the card over. It had a time on it.

She understood the message. Peterson wanted to speak to her alone.

Shifting to slide it into the pocket of her jeans, she reached behind her neck to undo the sling. The damn thing was more annoying than helpful and the ache in her shoulder had turned into a constant burn. They'd given her painkillers, but she hated to feel muddled.

Flexing her right hand, she tested her mobility and the sting traveled all the way down to her fingers. She had a couple of days to get it back, but for now, this would have to do.

"You should put the sling back on," Richard chided as he returned, three pizza boxes in hand. He stacked them onto the coffee table. "What do you want to drink?"

"Water is fine." She didn't need any alcohol, not on top of the anesthetic or if she ended up having to take one of those damn pain pills to placate Richard. The fact that she wanted to erase the worry in his eyes worried her. The deeper she went down this rabbit hole, the more it would hurt to extract herself.

He returned from the kitchen with plates, paper towels and two bottles of water. Setting it out, he turned and scooped her up before settling back onto the sofa with her in his lap.

"Richard, this violates the twelve-inch rule," she reminded him and tried to ignore just how nice it was to be in his lap with his body curved around hers. She'd never craved protection before, but damn if he didn't make it nice.

"Shh, I'm being impossible." His arms tightened around her. "And I need a minute to make sure you're all right." Touched by the rough emotion in his voice, she leaned into him and brushed her fingers down his cheek.

"I am all right. It's really a scratch."

"It could have been a lot worse." He studied her and the deep brown of his eyes seemed to have darkened to black.

"But it wasn't." She needed to soothe away his worry. "I'm fine. See? You can feel me. You're holding me and I'm okay."

"You know it's okay if you're not, right?" He tucked a finger under her chin and nudged her gaze up. "I get that you didn't cry because you're used to being the strong one, but it is okay if you were scared. Hell, I was terrified."

Most men would never admit that and her already tremendous respect for him inched up a notch. "I didn't have time to be afraid," she confessed. Ready to kick herself for allowing the distraction and giving that shooter the opportunity, yes. Afraid? No. But a lick of fear against her spine made a lie out of those words. She hadn't been afraid for herself at all—but the shooter hadn't wanted to kill her. Choking the thought off, she focused on him. "But I do need something."

"Anything." He brushed his fingers through her hair. She hadn't put it back up after the hospital, only taking the time at her apartment to comb it out.

"Food?" Distract him, get the worry out of his eyes and ease the guilt she could read in his troubled expression—that was her goal. "I'm starving."

Her stomach cooperated with the mission, growling as if to punctuate the demand, and his cheeks creased with a wide smile. "Food I can do." He let her go with some reluctance and set her down on the sofa next to him as though she were made of fine porcelain. After loading up the plates with pizza and opening her water bottle for her, he dragged a pillow over to set it on her lap like a makeshift table.

Violently aware of his gaze on her as she took a bite, she nodded to the television. "Movie?"

"It's late." He frowned. "You should get some rest."

"Are you ready to sleep?" Pushing aside her fatigue, she knew without asking he'd have trouble. He wore his concern like a hair coat and it would torture him if she didn't find a way for him to relax.

"No...any preference?" He twisted and found the remotes, flicking the television on, but muting it while he pulled up the guide.

"Find something you like," she suggested. God, she played with fire and would likely go straight to hell at this rate. "We're supposed to be getting to know each other, right?"

The slash of a grin softened the hard line of his jaw and the tension in his shoulders eased a fraction. "You have to promise not to laugh."

More curious than anything, she nodded. "Done." She took a bite of her pizza and watched as he switched the television over to a selection of films and in the list of most recently watched were legal films. She raised her eyebrows. He selected *A Time to Kill*.

"You watch movies about lawyers." She didn't laugh, but she had to bite the inside of her lip hard.

"Yes." He slid her a sideways glance. "What kind of movies do you like?"

"You can find out tomorrow when I pick." Because admitting her love for action movies with military themes might be a bit too revealing.

"Tease." But he grinned.

"Shut up and play the movie." *Before I make an even bigger mistake than I already have.* She wasn't supposed to be involved. Caring compromised her objectivity. But she suspected that it was too late. Settling back against the sofa, she tried to concentrate on the pizza and the movie. The quiet only served to heighten her awareness of the man next to her.

I'm already compromised...

~

SATURDAY MORNING DAWNED FAR TOO EARLY, but her shoulder's brutal ache dragged her out of sleep. Breathing through the throb, she took her time stretching each of her muscles. Richard had set her prescription bottles on the table next to the guest bed and, though he'd lingered, she'd managed to shoo him out of the room so she could get some sleep.

But the reluctance to send him away had become a palpable cramp in her stomach. Easing up, she flexed her right arm and damn if the bruised tissue didn't hurt worse than it had the day before. Adrenaline and shock were distant memories—stiffness was her worst enemy. Swinging her legs over, she bit down on a groan as pain stretched fire across her too tight muscles and skin.

A one-two knock announced Richard before he opened the door. "Hey, I was just coming by to see if you were awake and wanted some coffee." He'd crossed from the door to the bed and crouched in front of her in the time it took her to blow out a long hard breath. "You're hurting."

"It's a little sore," she admitted, but she kept flexing her hand, slowly and forcing the muscles to stretch a bit more each time. She couldn't afford to be too stiff and unfortunately, the best medicine was movement—no matter how unpleasant.

"You didn't take the pills the doctor gave you, did you?" Exasperation rode his words.

"No." She focused on him, dressed casually in a T-shirt and shorts. His attorney façade was nowhere to be seen. Instead, she was treated to long, lean muscles and dark, tanned skin with the lightest sprinkle of crisp hairs decorating his arms and down his legs. His very male presence definitely upset the equilibrium she struggled to maintain. "I don't like to be muddle headed."

Rather than chastise her, he rubbed his palm along her leg. She'd slept in a tank top and shorts and she'd never been so aware of the thinness of the cotton before. "How about I cut them in half? You can take smaller doses and gauge how foggy they make you feel?" Her surprise at the offer must have shown, because he gave her leg a gentle squeeze. "Worst part of my recovery? The pain meds. Made it hard to think, but pain *also* makes it hard to think. So I found that if I lowered the doses some, it helped alleviate the pain and I didn't feel like I'd come down with a case of stupid."

The corners of her mouth curved. Richard would not like to have his brain impaired. He may have made for a cute drunk, but she'd never doubted his mental acumen, not even then. Both alcohol and pain medication dulled reactions, but if her current struggle was any indicator, her reactions were already suffering. "Okay," she agreed. "Half the dose."

"Good girl." He patted her leg and her skin continued to tingle from his touch as he shifted to open the bottle and look at the prescription advice. Fortunately, they'd given her tablets. "I'll go cut these in half and get you some coffee."

"I can come down." Her synapses continued to fire in short, heady little bursts from his nearness and she curled her fingers into her palm to keep from testing the softness of the hair on his forearm. "You're all dressed." More than that, he had on shoes and a hint of aftershave.

"Woke up early," he admitted. "And I checked in on you, but—" he held up a hand when she raised her brows, "—I stayed by the door. Once I was up, I was up. Need a hand getting dressed?"

Ignoring the playful leer, she shook her head. "I can do it. What I'd really like is a shower, but they said twenty-four hours until I can change the bandage."

He leaned in and his breath tickled the side of her neck as he inhaled deeply. The sudden nearness and intimacy sent a pulse of need arcing from her breasts to her toes and back to pool in her middle. Strong, clean, masculine earthiness filled her nostrils and she wanted to drown in it. *I am so screwed.*

Drawing back, he gave her a lazy grin. "You smell sweet to me, so your shower can wait." The knowing look in his eyes said he hadn't missed an ounce of her reaction. "I'll wait for you in the hall."

She didn't move until the door clicked shut behind him. Glancing down, she stared at the hard points of her nipples clearly outlined by her thin tank top. "Sports bra," she muttered. "I need to sleep in one here."

Five minutes later, she changed her mind—the bra strap cut right across the slice on her shoulder and increased the pressure. Swearing, she rummaged around in her duffel until she found another tank top and layered the two. It wasn't much, but fortunately she'd never been gifted in the boob department.

Trading her sleep shorts for a pair of capris, she skipped shoes altogether. The last thing she wanted to ask Richard for was helping her tie the damn things. Cradling her arm to her chest, she paused in the bathroom to run a comb through her hair. Braiding it was out of the question and when she tried to lift her bad arm to put it in a ponytail, black spots danced in front of her eyes.

Leaving it down sent the wrong message, but her abdomen clenched in anticipation of his reaction. He'd been totally ignoring everything else in their contract save for the first part—*Richard must be impossible.* Tossing the comb down, she brushed her teeth and made a cursory wash of her face.

As promised, Richard waited in the hall. They went down together and she found a wide variety of donuts, muffins, bagels and fresh fruit along with coffee waiting in the kitchen. Eyeing the plethora of food, she chuckled.

"I wasn't sure what you'd like, so I got a little of everything," he admitted.

"And assumed that I can eat enough for a football team?" But she picked out a blackberry muffin and bit into it. It was still warm and tasted a little like heaven. Swallowing the bite, she eyed him. "You didn't go out and get these did you?"

"No, I sent one of Armand's goon squad to pick them up." He poured her a cup of coffee and slid the mug over before pulling out a cutting board and going to work on her pills.

"Richard?" They needed to address his attitude about security. "They're not bad guys. They just want to keep you safe."

He set one of the half pills on her plate and added the antibiotics next to it. "Individually, I'm sure they're fine. That said, I don't like being watched or under twenty-four-hour observation. They check out anyone who walks up to me, they know every detail of my day, and I can't breathe without them dogging every step. There's safe and there is living in a bubble." Irritation grated under his words and bitterness twisted his lips. "I had enough of that when the FBI watched us for three years, and interrogated everyone from my teachers to my friends to my neighbors."

"That had to suck," she said quietly and tried to ignore the guilt curdling in her stomach.

"More than I care to admit." He scrubbed a hand over his face. "I think that was actually the hardest part of my friendship with Armand to swallow."

"His security?"

"No. The lies about his security then, later, his security." Her heart stopped on the word *lies*, but she bit into the muffin and waited. Richard had walked over to the sink to wash off his knife and look out the window. "Do you know how I met him?"

She knew some of it. "In college. I thought around the same time he met Anna." Finishing the muffin, she washed down the last bite with a swallow of coffee.

"Take your pills. We'll go sit out by the pool and I'll tell you a story." A smile eased the fresh tension in his expression. "One very few people have ever heard."

"That sounds a little personal," she murmured. *Too personal.*

"But that's what this weekend is about." He

loaded up a plate with another selection of muffins, including two of the blackberry she'd eaten. When he stared at the pills on her plate, she sighed and popped both into her mouth.

"Have *you* taken your meds?" she countered.

"Yes, ma'am, before you got up. Now, grab your cup." He winked and added a carafe of the coffee to the tray he made up and his own coffee cup. Once poolside, the early morning breeze carrying the scent of the sea wrapped around them. She had to admit it was a lot nicer in the sun and stretched her legs out comfortably. Richard offered her sunglasses and she slid them on.

"You're spoiling me," she accused lightly. She needed to remember that this couldn't last. To not get attached. *Yeah, right.*

"I like spoiling you." He took a seat on the lounger opposite hers and freshened up the coffee cups. "So, Armand and I met during our freshmen year. We were actually assigned to be roommates."

Curious in spite of herself, she asked the first question that came to mind. "As a prince, I would have thought his security wouldn't want him sharing his room with a total stranger."

"He wasn't acting as a prince then, not yet. Armand told me later that his goal had been to have a *real* college experience—a real American one, anyway. Roommates were part of the package and most freshmen shared their dorm with three other guys. Somehow I thought I'd lucked out to split a room with only one. I found out later his guys were stationed in the room across from ours and the ones on either side. A detail of eight, I think he had. Two others roamed in and out, but the other six maintained pretty constantly—enrolled in classes and pretty much acting like other students."

"So you had no idea." That, she'd been well aware, had been the major bone of contention between the grand duke and his fiancée. Anna hadn't known about his royal heritage and when she did find out—*years* into their relationship—the lack of honesty split them up.

An ugly warning about paralleling that situation if ever there was one.

"None." He speared a strawberry and held it out to her. "Someone said these were her favorites."

Accepting the strawberry, she matched his grin. "Thank you."

"You're welcome." His gaze lingered on her mouth as she took a bite. It was the perfect mixture of sweet and tart and she couldn't help a little sigh. "And now I need to order you boxes more."

"Later." She accepted the offer graciously enough. "You were saying about the grand duke?"

"Call him Armand, at least between you and me." Richard picked up another muffin. "Because that's who he is. Anyway, that first couple of semesters he was a decent enough guy. Didn't make a big mess, pretty generous with the pizza, and he could always get beer—even if he preferred the snooty European brands." He broke the blueberry muffin in half and spread a little bit of butter on it. "We did well. He didn't party late and he never had a problem if I brought a girl back. I always returned the favor if he wanted to sneak Anna in."

Pausing, he considered the muffin and his grin turned self-deprecating. "Of course, I was a monk and only said I was sneaking a girl in if I needed to study." He dared a look at her as if to see if she bought it.

Amusement bubbled up through her and she laughed. "Of course you did."

"Good girl." He winked. "So we go through our freshmen year, just a couple of average guys, struggling with the course load, making friends, and you know...having that American dream." But his amusement sobered. "For me, it was a bit of a dream. I was a scholarship kid and what the scholarship didn't pay for, I took part time jobs to cover. I'd worked every summer I was in high school and saved up the money. Mom wouldn't have been able to afford it and I knew she had Barbara to worry about. Armand was loaded, but he never let on. He paid for more than his part, but he seemed normal—accent and all."

He finished the muffin and then used a napkin to wipe his hands. When he glanced at her coffee cup, she shook her head. The pain medication eased the constant throb beating in her shoulder in time to her pulse and the sun warmed her legs. Curling on her good side, she watched him. "So when did he tell you?"

"Right after our last final for the semester."

Leaning toward her, he rested his elbows on his knees and cradled his coffee cup. "Anna had a different schedule, but Armand and I had planned to hang out, grab a movie or something while he waited for her to finish. Instead, he brought a six pack and we found a quiet corner of the quad and he told me who he was."

"Was that weird for you?" She wanted to reach over and brush that lock of hair off his forehead again. To kiss away the tight lines from the corners of his eyes.

"Yeah. At first I thought he was just messing with me, but he gave me proof and while I sat there digesting that I, the scholarship kid and son of a felon, had just spent my entire first year in college rooming with a prince, he asked me for my advice." Richard shook his head and she could hear the notes of disbelief that harkened back to that long ago conversation. "He wanted to tell Anna, but he wasn't sure what she would do.

"I told him that everyone deserves the truth, but if he didn't think she could handle it—and if he wasn't prepared to lose her when she didn't— then maybe he shouldn't." The advice pinged against her heart. *Can you handle the truth of why I came to work for you?* "Not my finest hour and Armand was worried that knowing who he really was would change their relationship. He worried it would change ours too. As it turned out, title or not, he really was the same guy."

"I guess that's why you two have stayed best friends." It made sense—she'd seen the two men together. They communicated on a variety of levels and with a familiarity that bridged any social distinction.

"Mostly. Don't get me wrong, he can be a dick. Especially if he doesn't get his way. Man is a control freak, but he grew up in a world that demanded it of him. College was the one time I really saw him let go. After his father died and Anna left him, he was a different for too long." He sighed. "And while I want to kick his ass from here to next week for that security crap, I get why he does it."

"Easier to ask for forgiveness than seek permission?" She floated, a misty fine curtain draped over her. A half pill was way too much, but she was too relaxed to care.

"Something like that." He tipped his head. "You're slurring a little, you okay?"

"Sh-tupid pills." It sounded funny and she grinned. "Why don't you like his security?"

Richard's expression softened. He set his coffee cup aside then stood to open the large umbrella. Cooling shade spread over her. "I took a summer and traveled with him, got a real taste for his life. I couldn't take a piss without one of them being somewhere nearby and it brought up a lot of bad memories." Crouching next to her, he moved the coffee cup from her lax fingers. She watched him. It was a hell of a fight to keep her eyes open, but at least her shoulder didn't hurt. "I used to play cards with the guys and they lost a lot, but I made them a bet. If I could get away from them, they would have to pay up on what they owed. Otherwise, they wouldn't owe me a dime."

"Hmm, you got away didn't you?" She shook her head. Her Richard liked to win and when they'd been watching him, he'd watched them.

"Yes I did." His mouth curved. "Really pissed them off."

"Promise me you won't slip away this time?" She yawned and her eyes kept shutting no matter how hard she forced them back up. Some bodyguard she was—but then Richard hadn't brought her home to protect him. He didn't know it was her job. "Don't want you hurt."

"I'm not going anywhere." He stroked her cheek. "Go to sleep, honey. I'll make sure you don't burn and we can talk more when you wake up." He might have said something else, but she floated away to the soft, masculine sound of his voice.

CHAPTER 9
RICHARD

Watching her sleep fascinated him in a way that bordered on obsessive. Richard had to drag his attention away. Checking the umbrella to make sure she stayed in the shade, he carried the food tray back inside and put up their breakfast. Morning papers tucked under his arm, he was about to head back out to the pool when his cell phone vibrated in his pocket.

The number was one of the security detail. "Yes?" he answered and walked to the front door to check the gate via the window.

"Mr. Prentiss, we have a Benedict Prentiss at the gate. According to the notes from your assistant, you have a restraining order in place. He insists it's important, however. How do you wish us to proceed?"

"Keep him there."

"Yes, sir."

Richard tossed the papers down on a table and walked back to the pool. Kate lay on her side, face pillowed against her good hand, sound asleep.

Did he want to see his father?

Not particularly.

His gut clenched the moment he'd recognized his father's voice in the outer office. It had been nearly ten years since Benedict's last attempted contact and Richard had had to bodily throw him out of Barbara's apartment.

His sister had moved to London shortly thereafter and Richard filed for the restraining orders to keep the man away from the rest of his family. It had broken his mother's heart, but he'd convinced her in the same ruthless fashion he'd tackled every business deal before or since. Benedict Prentiss cared about one person—himself. The government never recovered the money he'd stashed away and Richard had endured more than one tax audit over the last few years as a result.

Even understanding *why* the government kept a stern eye on him didn't ease the fuming resentment in his soul. The front desk at his building had mentioned his father had tried to access his office floor several times since the scene in Kate's office, but they'd declined him admittance. Richard knew why.

Kate'd handled it for him so he didn't have to. She'd never breathed a word about it, never asked him for any explanations and, until his overindulgence with the wine, they hadn't broached the topic. The woman had rapidly found a foothold in his heart and he was hard-pressed to see any reason why he should keep holding back purely for professional reasons.

Wanting her was the sweetest torture he'd ever suffered.

Sliding his phone back into his pocket, he walked back to the door and headed for the gate. His father's car sat, engine off, on the other side. Two of the security guards flanked him. Benedict walked up to the wrought iron as Richard approached from the opposite side.

Stopping a good foot away, he slid his hands into his pockets and nodded to the men. They backed off a discreet distance, then Richard focused on his father. "What do you want?"

"Richie, is that any way to speak to your father?" The bravado in his voice said one thing, but the sad, defeated look in his father's eyes told a different story.

"No one calls me that anymore. You have..." He pulled his hand out of his pocket and checked the time on his watch. "Five minutes."

"You're not going to let me in?" His father had always been a big man and, in his childhood, Richard imagined his father was secretly one of those lumberjacks with his booming voice and broad shoulders. It seemed possible that his father carried the weight of the world up there. His charm, even at the height of his trials for fraud and embezzlement, could never be denied. It was how he'd parted many of his victims from their hard-earned cash.

People wanted to trust him.

Hell, Richard had worshipped him.

He'd also had a front row seat to the havoc and destruction caused by one man's charm and lies. "No, you're fine right where you are and now you have four minutes and thirty seconds."

"We didn't raise you to be rude." The snapped admonishment was laughable.

"You didn't raise me at all. Four minutes and ten seconds." He returned his hands to his pockets, it helped maintain a cool head and the gate was for his father's protection. If it opened, Richard might very well punch the old man in the face.

And he wasn't worth that kind of aggravation.

Rubbing a hand against his jaw, Benedict Prentiss took another step toward the gate. Oddly enough, today he appeared lucid and sober—a far cry from the disheveled drunk that had stormed into Richard's office. "I want to apologize to you."

"All right." Because after all these years, what was an apology worth?

"Dammit, Richie, I know I screwed up. I screwed up a lot, but you and Barb—you're all I have. Your mother won't speak to me, won't take my calls, and that new husband of hers? He's as bad as you are. Won't let me take a step on the property or pass on my messages."

Richard had always been fond of Carlisle Jackson. Looking back on it, their benefactor had been interested in his mother from the beginning, but Jennifer Prentiss had loved her first husband and remained ridiculously loyal through not one disaster, but two. Jackson gave his mother a job, helped send her back to school, and he'd settled rather comfortably into the role of friend.

Divorced before Richard went to high school, his mother hadn't dated and Richard still recalled his graduation day. Carlisle had taken him aside and asked him, man-to-man, would Richard object if Carlisle took his mother on a date. He'd been patient for years, and he'd been a damn good stand-in for the idiot in front of Richard now.

"Benedict..." Because he didn't deserve to be called Father, much less Dad. "You are not allowed to be within one hundred feet of her. That's what the restraining order is for. If you came here to complain, I'm done."

"No, that's not why I'm here." He reached out to grip the iron bars between them and Richard studied his sallow, faintly yellow complexion.

"You're sick." *Son of a bitch.* "You didn't come here to make apologies or amends. You've been trying to get ahold of me and Barbara because you're sick."

The older man's shoulders slumped. "Yes, I'm sick, but I do want to tell you I'm sorry. I'm sorry I screwed up our lives and I'm sorry for what I did to you kids. You shouldn't have had to... You shouldn't have had to grow up with a father like me."

"Well, we didn't. You made sure of that." Richard shook his head. "But you don't get it. You're sorry *now*. Because you're sick, because

167

you're dying and alone. That was your choice, you made that bed. Now you can lie in it."

He pivoted to walk away, then paused before storming back to the gate and pinning his father with a glare. "Are you sorry for all the other lives you ruined? For the money you took and never gave back? Are you sorry for all the nights Mom cried herself to sleep because Barb wanted her daddy? Are you sorry that the FBI tore our lives apart to find out where you hid the money you stole? Or because thirty years later they still keep an eye on me in case I have some of your money? Are you sorry for that?" Richard wanted to throttle him.

Benedict couldn't hold Richard's gaze and looked down. "You made a good life for yourself, Richie. I'm proud of you. I won't come back, if that's what you want."

Refusing to be sucked into the pity party the old man was throwing, Richard nodded. "That's exactly what I want." Transferring his attention to the security men, he had to appreciate their lack of expression as they watched the argument. "He's leaving now. Don't ever admit him and you don't have to call up and let me know he's here." The last was for his father's benefit.

Turning his back on Benedict, Richard strode up the driveway and inside before he could change his mind. If for one instant he thought his father really had achieved an epiphany and was willing to turn his life around.

Slamming the door behind him, he paused to lean his head and fist against it. Nothing his father ever said would be worth listening to. He wanted to pound something until his knuckles were raw and bloody. Any other time, he'd have picked up the phone and called Armand—they could hit the racquetball court. *But Kate...*

Lifting his head, he glanced toward the pool. *Kate's here.*

The roiling black cloud of anger dissipated and he scooped up his papers and walked to look at the clear blue water. She was awake and on the phone. Sliding the glass door open, he leaned out and her sleepy smile soothed the bruised ache in his heart.

"No, sir. Like I said, I didn't see the plate. I think the most remarkable thing about the sedan was that it wasn't remarkable."

Frowning, he stepped out and shut the door behind him before walking over to join her. Ducking under the umbrella, he sat on the lounger next to her.

"I understand that." She gave him another smile, then sighed as she listened to whomever was on the phone. "Yes, if I can think of anything else, I will call. Yes—no. I don't know if we're going into the office on Monday. I would presume so." She shot him a questioning look and he nodded.

Who the hell was asking her about their—

Peterson.

Richard held his hand out and her brows went up. "Let me talk to him," he said, loud enough for the man on the other end to hear.

She handed over the phone, but he read her reluctance. "Peterson?"

"Yes, Mr. Prentiss. I apologize, I wanted to go over the details one more time with Miss Braddock after she'd had a chance to rest."

"Well if you need to talk to her again, you can call me. Otherwise, she's taking the rest of the weekend off. Have a good day." He hung up without waiting for the man to respond.

"Someone's testy." Kate rubbed a hand against her face and smothered a yawn. "Sorry I fell asleep on you."

"Sorry I wasn't here to keep the phone from waking you up. How's the shoulder?"

"Achy, but not bad." He loved how husky her voice went and the soft expression on her face. It was an enticingly new picture of her.

"Good and ignore Peterson if he calls you back. They can direct their security inquiries through me." For once, he didn't mind the idea of being barricaded in his house. At least he had Kate to share it with.

"I'm your assistant," she pointed out, dry humor in her smile.

"Not this weekend you're not." A fact for which he was profoundly grateful. "This weekend you're my guest and I'm your host."

"You realize that saying it doesn't make it so." Her resistance was back, her spirit seemed to have rebounded from the numb state of the painkillers and she appeared to be shedding the shock from the day before.

"Truth is found in perception. If you say a

thing enough times, people will start to believe it." He tossed down the verbal gauntlet.

"That's a purely philosophical argument. I can say I'm your guest until we're blue in the face, but come Monday morning we go back to the old labels."

"Maybe," he countered.

"What? If we get involved then you fire me?" Amusement filled her eyes. She didn't believe him.

Not yet.

"Or maybe you quit—though I really hope you don't. I like working with you." Oddly enough, he recognized a great deal of truth in that statement. He'd worked with Miranda for years. They'd been a well-oiled machine, but at the end of the day, she went back to her life and Richard to his. In the intervening weeks since her departure he hadn't really missed her.

He'd miss Kate.

"You can't have it both ways," she argued and his grin grew.

"Why not?" After all, it was his job to be impossible. It said so in their contract.

THEY'D RETREATED indoors after lunch and, to his delight, Richard found out that not only did Kate know how to play video games—she was damn good at them. Several rounds of *Call of Duty* put their debate on the backburner and he hadn't laughed so hard in a long time. When she'd excused herself to shower, he went out to fire up the grill and get the steaks ready to cook.

A night on the deck, under the stars, with some real food and maybe a glass or two of merlot—*well, with her meds, maybe water but we'll still have a good time.* Stacking up the steaks neatly and wrapping the potatoes in foil, it occurred to him he'd been laughing all afternoon.

He'd relaxed.

His father, the shooting, the upcoming contract negotiations, his pending cases—they'd all gone on the backburner. He'd had fun. Grinning at the realization, he checked the bins in the fridge for tomatoes and lettuce. He could toss a salad after the steaks were grilled.

"Richard?" Her voice drifted down the stairs. He left the food on the counter and walked around the corner to look up.

"You okay?" He started to climb the steps, then paused when he realized she was only in a towel again. White cotton had never looked so good.

"I'm a little embarrassed, but otherwise fine." She retreated a few steps. Her long hair hung damply down her back.

Continuing up the stairs, he kept his gaze on her face because he'd already gotten a glimpse of her legs and, while the towel covered a hell of a lot more than the swimsuit, it was only one tug away. "What's up?"

Turning around, she showed him the bandage. "I can't get it off. I think it's the angle, but I wanted to change it."

Understanding kicked his rising temperature down a notch and he motioned for her to precede him. "Got the rest of the stuff in your room?"

"Yeah, I can put it back on."

"Don't worry about it. This definitely falls under the *I get to take care of you* part of our quid pro quo." A certain amount of satisfaction flowed through him because she'd *asked* him. Yes, she had tried to do it on her own, but when she needed help, she asked him.

So I help her change the bandage and then I go back down and fix dinner. It demonstrates I'm a good guy even when I'm impossible.

He followed her into the room and through it to the bathroom. The air was steamy from the shower. Vanilla and juniper filled his nostrils and it was liked being wrapped up in the warm, damp heat of her. The thought went straight to his groin and his cock stiffened uncomfortably.

"The stuff is here." She tapped the fresh bandages and tape on the counter along with the antibiotic ointment they'd given her at the hospital.

Sucking in another lungful of her sweet, feminine scent, Richard forced himself to focus on the task at hand. "This might sting when I pull it off."

"I'm all about ripping the Band-Aid off." Tough and beautiful, she never failed to impress him. She resettled her stance and braced her good hand on the counter. "Do it."

Wiping his palms against his shorts, he closed the distance between them. Her gaze met his in the still foggy mirror and Richard smiled. "You're gorgeous, you know that?"

The corner of her mouth tilted. "I have wet, stringy hair and I'm wearing a towel. I hardly think that qualifies."

"Oh." He traced a finger across her shoulder and gathered up the wet mass to push it out of his way. "I think it more than qualifies. When you're all glammed up, you're stunning, but I think I like you like this best."

"Okay, I'll bite. Why?"

All of his blood went south at the word "bite" and he traced the base of her "creek-dogging" scar. It went down farther than he'd realized, all the way to the bottom of her shoulder blade. It must have been a hell of a cut.

"Warm, soft and damp from the shower?" He dipped his head, giving into temptation and pressed his lips to the flutter of her pulse. The catch of her breath encouraged him and he nibbled another soft kiss. She tasted sweet and her heart began to race, the erratic beat going crazy beneath his lips.

"Richard..." The strained note in her voice elongated the syllables in his name and he bit gently on her skin, sucked lightly and she swayed. Closing his hand around her good shoulder, he held her steady and continued to kiss his way up to her jaw. Kate's head fell back and Richard sealed the last few inches between them so she could rest her head against his shoulder. Her wet hair dampened his shirt, but he continued his leisurely exploration of her jaw. The nibbling little touches brought his need to a fever pitch.

Tracing his fingers up her arm, he adored the softness of her skin and the supple muscles contracting under the contact. She turned her head and her mouth parted. He took the invitation, branding her into his blood, and savored the long, thorough exploration complete with teasing swipes of her tongue.

She moaned and the sound vibrated through him. Biting down on her lower lip, he held his hips still when her sweet bottom rubbed against his cock and every molecule in his body strained toward her. Sliding his hand to the nape of her neck, he held her and deepened the kiss further.

When she moaned again, he ripped off the bandage.

Her gasp came sharp and hot against his lips and he took another long thorough kiss before letting them both up for air. The golden glints in her wide eyes glimmered at him and a pink flush spread across her cheeks. But her mouth—God, her lips were slick and wet and swollen.

Nipping her lower lip, he whispered. "You need to look at the mirror again."

"Why?" The dazed sound stroked his ego and his smile grew. She was not remotely immune to him. Good because his body practically screamed for hers.

"Because I need to check your stitches and put a fresh bandage on." He held up the other one. "I think I can really get behind this ripping the Band-Aid off method." The flush on her cheeks spread and to his absolute delight, her ears went red. The rise and fall of her breasts attracted his attention and he reached down and carefully pulled the towel back up.

"And you should hold this tighter." He deserved a fucking medal for his restraint. Disposing of the bandage, he gave her a moment to gather herself then checked her stitches. It was an ugly mottling of black and blue, the skin held together by two tightly woven bits of surgical thread. A bit swollen, but otherwise clean, he took gentle care in applying the ointment around, but not on the stitches before he added the clean bandage and tape.

Pressing a kiss to the top of her shoulder, he glanced up to meet the wide-open curiosity in her gaze via the mirror. "You good?"

"You're amazing," she whispered and his face heated at the quiet sincerity in her words. "I've never met anyone like you."

"Good." He leaned down and rested his cheek against hers, a wave of possessiveness overtaking him. "Because I feel the same way about you." Instead of pulling away, she relaxed against him. Something deep inside him eased at the show of trust. "You should get dressed. I'm going to cook you a fantastic dinner and we're going to talk."

She stared at him steadily, then nodded. "Okay."

"And, Kate?" He turned and pressed her lips against the side of her head. "The door on my side? It's wide open. You think about it."

He left her alone and headed back down the

stairs. His cock would have a zipper imprint in it after that kiss, but, all seduction aside, he wanted the cool rational woman to want him every bit as much as her feminine soft and melting counterpart had in that bathroom.

She'd come alive in his arms and her kiss had turned fierce, as demanding and giving as his own. If he'd pushed it, they could be naked right now—of that he had no doubt.

Yes, he had her body, but he wanted her mind and that took a whole new level of seduction.

Whistling, he set the potatoes into the preheated oven and pulled out the salad fixings to chop and toss.

CHAPTER 10

KATE

For seven long minutes after Richard strolled out the door, Kate stood in the bathroom and tried to get her rebellious heart under control. Heat flushed her face and her skin tingled with the memory of everywhere he'd touched her.

I can't keep doing this.

She'd liked the man well enough when she'd gone to work for him, but with every minute she spent with him—every day—that like grew to respect and caring. He worked his ass off for his clients, he was a damn good friend to the grand duke and he didn't take advantage of his position unless someone tried to cut it out from under him.

No, he was a good guy and he didn't deserve the lies. Still in the towel, she walked into her borrowed room and picked up her cell phone. When Peterson had phoned and woken her up from the painkiller-induced nap earlier, she'd

179

given him a status report. He'd called her on her level of involvement and warned her about the danger in taking the relationship too far.

She'd been unable to respond because Richard walked back out onto the deck. What the hell would she have said? *No, I know fucking the grand duke's best friend wasn't in the plan, but my protectee started it, so suck it up?* Perching on the edge of the bed, she stared at her phone.

They'd had a hell of a lot of fun. She adored it when he cut loose and relaxed. Remembering how she'd melted against him and the hard strength enveloping her as he seduced her senses —his ripping the bandage off hadn't stung nearly as much as it might have. Riding an endorphin high, she hadn't cared about the towel slipping, either.

Hell, half of her mind had already taken the next leap forward—dropping the towel and turning into him. She wanted to explore his body —find out what would make his pulse quicken, his body shake—and she wanted to have sex with him. Once would never be enough.

I'm falling for him.

At some point in the last few weeks—and she couldn't pinpoint when it happened—he'd stopped being her protectee and had become so much more.

When the shots had been fired, all she could think about was keeping him alive because losing him would kill her.

Unlocking her phone, she dialed the tower and waited for Peterson to answer.

"Braddock?" Cool, professional and controlled, Peterson had always been a master of efficiency. He'd entrusted her with not one, but two, protectees and he'd invested in her based on the recommendation of an old friend. She'd always be grateful for that.

"You were right," she said softly. "I have been compromised. Due to that, I am resigning my position for His Highness."

"We can replace you," Peterson said evenly. "Extract and send in another."

"No extraction required." She didn't want to leave Richard. "But I can't continue as his bodyguard." Sucking in her first deep breath in days, relief left her shaky and the noose around her neck loosened.

"Resigning your post does not relieve you of the agreements you signed." He referred to the agreement stipulating the disclosure of any activities she'd performed in service to the Andraste family, specifically in their security detail.

"I understand, but as of...five minutes ago, I am done."

"Kate." Peterson shifted gears. "The threat is a real one and it's still out there."

"I know." So very aware of it, in fact. "I'm not going to *not* protect him. I just won't do it on the grand duke's payroll anymore."

"What if someone shoots at him again?" Worry coated the words and she heard his underlying concern.

"I don't need a paycheck to want him alive,

Peterson. Please express my regrets to His Highness. And a request?"

"Which is?"

"When we wrap this up, when we find the shooter, I need permission to tell Richard I worked for the grand duke." He deserved to know the whole of it. She could tell him why she'd started working for him. He was a man who needed honesty and she wanted him to have it.

"I will pass on the request. Be careful. Kate—" He hesitated and she thought he was done when she heard the squeak of an office wheel and Peterson blew out a breath. "It's harder to protect someone you love than you may realize. You can get wrapped up in them and miss something when it does go wrong."

"I know." She'd have a split-second to respond to the threat. "I won't let him down. Thanks for understanding."

"Be careful. As of this moment, you're still the subject of a security detail. Let the others take point."

Agreeing wasn't as hard as she'd thought it might be. That detail's job was to keep Richard alive. "I'm not the target. Remind them to protect Richard first."

They spoke for another minute and when she hung up she let out a long, trembling breath. She couldn't dive any further into this relationship as the servant of two masters—and only a fool would try to deny the very real chemistry consuming all the air between her and her *former* protectee.

Grinning, she bounced to her feet, not even the sting in her shoulder diminishing her good mood. She took her time in selecting a comfortable pair of denim shorts and a body-hugging tank top. To hell with the bra. Returning to the bathroom, she used a comb and blow dryer to tame the mass, which she left down. Richard liked it down. Eyeing herself in the mirror, she added a little lip gloss and grinned.

He wanted to play? He wouldn't know what hit him.

Humming, she strolled out of the room barefoot and padded down the stairs, clearing the last step with a hop. Following the scent of cooking meat, she found Richard manning the grill. The table on the upper part of the pool deck had been set for two and music filtered through the speakers hidden in the eaves of the deck cover.

Recognizing a familiar tune, she couldn't stop her grin. With the breeze coming in off the ocean and the sun slanting down over it, the entire set up promised romance and seduction. He'd declared his intentions and armed his theater of war. Being the target of so much effort had never happened to her before, and damn if her stomach didn't quiver and her heart skip a beat.

Letting herself out, she met his heated gaze when he glanced over his shoulder and skimmed his gaze over her. The caress of his attention was an invitation to join him. Padding across the sun-warmed wood, she paused at the table and spotted the bottles of water in a tub of ice and the wine—an Inglenook Cabernet

Sauvignon. He'd opened the bottle to let it breathe.

Pouring two glasses a quarter full each—she wasn't taking another one of those damn pain pills—she set the bottle down and carried the two glasses to the grill. "It smells wonderful." She kept her attention on him as she passed over his glass.

He eyed hers curiously and swept his gaze up to meet her eyes. "You sure?" Laden with so many meanings, the two very simple words packed a punch.

"To open doors," she toasted and his grin grew wider, creasing his face in delight. Her breath hitched because the man had no idea of the devastating effect he had on her equilibrium.

"To open doors," he murmured and their glasses clinked together. They both sipped, but he kept watching her.

"And to not burning these beautiful steaks you're preparing." Pleasure twisted in her chest at his muttered oath. He handed her back the wine glass before flipping the steaks.

In addition to the meat, he had created a foil pan on the top burner with onions, asparagus and peppers grilling together over the heat. The combination of scents made her hungry, but it was the man, not the wine, who intoxicated her most.

"How is your shoulder?" He cast her a side-long look and took his wine glass back.

"Can't feel a thing." It wasn't a lie. Beyond a twinge, she couldn't care less about the ache.

Since he wasn't touching the grill, she gave into the impulse and traced her fingers down the line of his arm. The tiny hairs tickled her skin. It didn't take much of a leap to imagine how sensuous it would be to rub against him. Her nipples tightened at the thought.

"Really? So would you say it's a temporary reprieve or result of the care you've received?" Another question lurked beneath the surface and she spread her hand over his shoulder and stroked the cottony softness of his shirt.

"Hmm. Hopefully not temporary, but then I have a very high threshold for pain. This tiny ache certainly can't compete with my other needs." She tipped the glass up for another drink. His throat bobbed with a swallow and she hid a smile. "Did I mention that this is a wonderful wine? The fruit is very evident in it."

"You did say you loved fruit and, of our local vintages, this is one of my favorites. The licorice and cloves are subtle, but they bring out the bite in the grapes."

Of course he knew about wine, the man was perfect.

Kate laughed. "Well, we've exhausted what I know about wine." Dragging her hand off him, she padded lazily to the rail and glanced out over the ocean. "So..."

"Yes?" He didn't follow her, but the weight of his gaze scorched her senses.

"Are you enjoying being impossible?" Twisting to lean against the rail, she drank in the view of him. His dark eyes, the way the wind tugged at his hair, and that damn lock of hair that continued to drift down onto his forehead. She loved that stupid little lock of hair. It made him look younger, easing the hard planes of his face, and transformed him from good-looking to breathtakingly handsome.

Someone could write a book about a man like him. Blunt, forceful and wielding charm the way others did sarcasm. The corner of his mouth quirked and a devilish glint gleamed in his eyes. "You're trying to seduce me."

"Am I?" She might never win a war of words with him, but damn would she have fun trying.

"So it would seem. Or perhaps it is merely a distraction to throw me off my game?" He flipped the steaks and checked the veggies. The heat from the grill left a primal shimmer of sweat on his skin.

"Could you truly be distracted from an impossible seduction by a counter of seduction?" Swirling the wine in her glass, she considered the possibilities. "Isn't that like fighting fire with more fire?"

"An effective technique if you have a range fire you can't control. You start a backfire and consume all the fuel in front of it so that when the two fires collide..." He clucked his tongue.

"I'm sorry, Richard. Are you trying to tell me that if we collide, you're going to fizzle out?"

Surprise blustered across his face and his eyes narrowed. For a split-second, she thought not only had she scored a point, she'd won the match, but he recovered. "I can assure you I don't *fizzle* out of anything."

"Well, that's very good to know, but we may have to test that theory later." They locked gazes and her body pulsed with the naked desire in his eyes. "For now, you need to feed me. I think we'll need all the caloric intake we can manage."

It was an offer.

He didn't answer right away, his attention dipped to the food he cooked then one by one, he removed the pair of steaks and added the veggies to the platter. The silence dragged on long enough that worry began to nibble on her spine. Shutting off the grill, he carried the platter and his wine glass to the table and set them down. Turning, his lashes swept up and he gave her a lingering look from head to toe.

Extending his hand, a smile full of dark promises curved his mouth. "Then would you allow me the honor of feeding you?"

That was an acceptance.

Her stomach bottomed out. She'd been calmer about jumping out of planes. Fear and nerves had never made her balk before and tonight would not be the exception. Pushing away from the railing, she sauntered toward him. "Open door?" she murmured, sliding her hand into his.

"I'll take the damn thing off its hinges." Then his mouth closed over hers, his tongue gliding over the seam of her lips demanding access, and she sighed. The passion in his touch sought acceptance and when she acquiesced, he swept in and claimed. It was the sweetest form of surrender and she moaned when he lifted his head. "But first?" He kissed the tip of her nose. "Calories. Lots of calories."

Laughter bubbled up inside her and she grinned. "Promise me there's dessert."

"Oh." He stroked the curve of her neck and if she'd been a cat, she would have purred. "There will definitely be dessert."

DINNER TURNED out to be fun and Richard took tormenting her to impossible levels—exactly as he was supposed to, he'd teased when she complained. The food was delicious—the baked potatoes soft and buttery, the steak damn near perfection, and the grilled veggies the excellent complement. They both nursed their wine, loosening up to only have a second half glass.

She wanted her wits about her and, evidently, so did he. "Out of curiosity..." He speared a pepper on his fork. "Why work as an assistant? You've got the drive and the capability to run your own small empire."

Fortunately, she didn't have to play a complicated word game to answer his question. "I never went to college," she admitted and his brows raised. "What, you thought only people who get a four-year degree are savvy?"

"Not at all, it's just surprising. You're wildly intelligent." The emphasis he put on the last two words delighted her more than if he'd called her beautiful. Of course, he'd done that too.

"Admittedly, I thought about it. But I was an army brat, I went army."

"You were—son of a bitch, no wonder you're so good at *Call of Duty*." Admiration and exasperation mingled in his laughter. "I think that's cheating. And more than a little sexy."

"Well, I was a communications specialist, not as sexy as you might think." She lifted her wine glass for a sip. "I spent six years in the service and got a lot accomplished, but after the boys, well, Mom was happier when I took a step back."

"So, you didn't want to leave?" He settled back in his chair, one foot braced against a rung on the bottom of hers.

"I wasn't a lifer." She shook her head. "It wasn't something I saw myself doing until retirement. I wanted to serve, I wanted to learn and I got a hell of an education. If you ever need me to take apart your electronics and put them back together, that I can do. If you need me to jump out of a plane and land on a deserted isle somewhere and set up a cell tower?" She grinned. "That I can do too."

"You just get sexier by the minute. You can para jump?" At her nod, he picked up his wine glass. "What else can you do that I don't know about?"

Since that skated perilously close to a truth she couldn't tell him yet, she danced along the edge. "I'm sure I have many hidden talents. What about you? What's the craziest thing you've ever done?"

"Probably playing hide and seek with Armand's security detail."

"How so?" She was curious, particularly in light of their current situation.

"Because I jumped out of a moving car and landed in an alley. Then I got lost in a street fair where I didn't speak the language." Boyish chagrin warmed his expression. "The secret of why they couldn't find me? I was well and truly turned around. I spent most of the day trying to figure out where the hell I was so I could get back."

"And you never told them because...?"

"Pride. Guilt." He spread his hands. "But I'd also made my point so the little impetuous action served its purpose. What about you? You jump over bridges and out of planes, but what's the craziest thing you've ever done?"

That didn't explain how he slipped them now, but they had time for that. Gritting her teeth, she made a face and stared at the pool "Would you believe me if I said that I've been pursued by a prince before?"

He leaned forward and put the wine glass down. "If his last name sounds anything like Dagmar, I don't want to know."

"No." She softened the response and covered his hand with hers. "I hadn't met His Highness before I started working for Anna." Which was the absolute truth. She'd worked for Peterson, taken on some jobs here and there when he'd had work for her, but not for the grand duke.

"All right." Richard relaxed and blew out a breath. "So what prince pursued you?"

"His name was Achmed Al-Sabah. He was the fourteenth son or something like that." She stroked her tongue against her teeth. Richard seemed relaxed, but she recognized the sharp look in his gaze. He wanted details. "I met him while on assignment in Kuwait. I'd gone there to do some work on one of our bases—which is neither here nor there—but he had been part of a tour. He saw me, decided I would make a fantastic princess, and began to send me the craziest things." No matter how entertained she was by the story, she never forgot how damn irritating it had been at the time.

"For example?" Richard curved his hand around hers, his thumb tracing a lazy pattern against skin. Tiny electric shocks impeded her interest in telling the story.

"First, he sent me silks—several thousand dollars' worth of silk. I wore fatigues and BDUs, not silk. The guys in my unit got a big laugh out of it. Then he sent me meals, gourmet meals flown in from all over the world, and he tried to send in a chef, but the gate guards wouldn't admit him to the base." She'd almost forgotten about her royal stalker. "Every gift included an invitation, usually something innocuous—a walk together, a supper, twice he invited me the palace. I declined every invitation, but when he sent me the camels? That I had to explain to my C.O."

Whether it was the consternation in her tone or the content of the statement, Richard laughed. "Camels?"

"A *dozen* camels." She squeezed his hand.

"And what offer did he have with the camels?"

"Oh, that was a proposal." Shaking her head, Kate laughed. "My C.O. told me we needed to put an end to the pursuit immediately and that meant letting the prince know in no uncertain terms that I wasn't interested, but..." She trailed off invitingly.

"There's always a but." He leaned forward, elbows on the table and played with her hand between his. "You couldn't upset the political balance or curry disfavor?"

"Exactly. So how does one tell a prince to stuff his camels up his ass politely?" She waggled her brows and Richard's grin grew.

"Very carefully."

"Well, that's one theory." She'd been polite. It hadn't worked. "You see, I had been gracious in declining every single gift. We'd sent them all back. I couldn't accept them and I'd always gotten someone from the public relations office to give me a very well-worded, cordial no, but they were all nos. Seriously I think this guy was just messing with me because he could. So, I asked my C.O. for a pass to go off base for thirty-six hours."

"Why?" He was completely hooked on the

story and, despite his constant caresses, she enjoyed his reactions too much to leave him hanging.

"Because I needed to give the army as much plausible deniability in my choices as I could. My C.O. approved it, but I had to take one of the MPs with me—Messer, he was a good guy. He played it cool and off we went to have lunch with a prince."

"Okay, now I'm intrigued. How the hell is going to lunch with that camel salesman going to send a message?" The protectiveness in his voice and grip turned fierce.

Rubbing her thumb against his fingers, she shushed him. "Shh, it's all right. I'm a big girl. I could handle it."

"Just because you can doesn't mean you should. No means no in any language." Hmm, probably a very good thing Richard hadn't been in her life during that particular episode. She rather suspected he'd have made an international incident. When she said as much he nodded firmly. "Damn straight. And I have a grand duke in my corner, he'd have helped."

"Well do you want to hear the rest of the story or would you like to get angrier on my behalf?" She lifted his hand to her lips and kissed his knuckles. "You're very sexy when you're angry."

The quiet fury in his gaze drained away and the want returned. "Finish, I'll behave."

"Hopefully not for long." His eyes flared at her tease, so she grinned and continued. "Lunch turned out to be a huge formal affair with a dozen of his closest relatives and, of course, Messer and me. We went through all the motions and then went for a long walk and Messer—acting as my 'brother'—informed the prince that his pursuit had earned a measure of interest from my 'family,' but unfortunately, we had rules and traditions that had to be observed."

Richard's attention remained riveted on her. "I think we're getting to the crazy part."

"Uh huh." She laughed. "The prince said he would happily meet any ritual my brother wanted to put him through to prove his great and undying love for me. Messer told him that in order for the family to feel comfortable accepting his pledge, he'd have to beat me in a hand-to-hand fight."

"What?" Richard stared.

"That was exactly what the prince said. He was shocked, I tell you, shocked, that combat was what was required. Now I had to stay quiet through all of this, demure and restrained and not laugh my butt off at his facial expressions. Messer told him that we came from a long line of warriors—technically true since he was my army brother. Anyway—" she pressed on before Richard could interrupt, "—the prince was outraged, but Messer gave him a helpless look and said if the prince didn't think he could handle a mere woman in a very straightforward fight, he could hardly be expected to protect and care for me in a manner that would be expected."

"Oh my God, he played him." Richard looked

torn between horror and amusement. Covering his mouth with one hand, he stared at her. "And what did this paragon do?"

"He argued for a little while, but finally conceded that, yes, he wanted me enough that he was willing to beat me to have me."

"Please tell me you kicked his ass?"

"All over the floor. We kept the fight very private—Messer with me and one of the prince's bodyguards with him. The bodyguard was ordered to stay out of it and so was Messer. After he was done puking in the corner, the prince offered me his most sincere apologies, but he'd changed his mind and dropped his pursuit." Merriment danced through her. "We never heard another word—no censure, no political fallout. Achmed didn't want anyone to know."

"...that a gorgeous, talented woman kicked his ass." Richard laughed, his open joy delighting her more than recounting the story. "You're right, that's one of the craziest things I've ever heard and damn if I'm not proud of you."

Pleasure speared her at the words.

"Of course, I'm not going to fight you physically to win."

"No?" She challenged, brows raised.

"No." It was his turn to lift her hand to his lips. "What I will do is begin here at your hand and kiss each finger and then glide my tongue up the soft side of your arm to the crook of your elbow. I want to explore every inch of your skin. If you're still in the game at that point, I'll ease your shirt up, just enough to let my hand rest against your abdomen while I nuzzle the curve of your neck and then your jaw and finally tempt that gorgeous mouth of yours—" his voice dropped and her breath hitched, her humor melting into a pool of molten heat, "—with the slowest of caresses, I'll ease a hand around your breast..."

She shoved the chair back and stood. "You win."

The triumph in his smile took her breath away. "But I've only just gotten started."

CHAPTER II
RICHARD

"**S**tarted?" The word shuddered out of her. She moistened her lips and the glossy sheen invited him closer. From the moment she had come out onto the deck she'd been delighting him—first with her teasing play running her fingers up his arm and then with her blatant invitation about the need for calories. Dinner, though, dinner had been an utter pleasure. She'd dug into the food and ate it with a gusto that he could appreciate, not an ounce of trying to eat only the salad and ignoring the rest.

He'd never told anyone before about getting lost that day. They all thought it demonstrated just how clever he was and it had given him insight into how to elude personal security. For a brief moment, he'd almost added how he slipped them during his recovery and again earlier that morning, but with more recent events he didn't want to worry her. Even Armand had tried to get him to reveal exactly how he'd done it.

But Kate appreciated the irony and told him

the most fascinating story in return. They had time for other tales later.

"Yes, started." Standing, he closed the distance between them and ran a finger down the front of her tank top, pausing in the valley between her very much bra-free breasts. He'd thought so, but damned if he didn't like finding out. "See, I'd like to take this off and play with your breasts."

"O-okay." She brought her hands up to spread against his chest. Her strength, he never questioned, nor her competence. She'd demonstrated her fierce spirit over and over again and yet when he'd realized that bullet *hurt* her it reminded him that strong didn't mean invincible.

"This isn't business," he told her bluntly. "This isn't about a contract or a work ethic or anyone but you and me." He had no qualms about crossing the dividing line between business and pleasure—hell, he'd already crossed it. He wanted Kate, but having been on the receiving end of that clever mind of hers, he knew damn good and well he wanted her mind on the exact same page as her body.

"Okay," she repeated the two-syllable word with a shudder.

Curling his finger around the fabric, he stroked the soft skin from the curve of her shoulder blade to the top of one breast. "Is it okay for me to use my fingers to touch?"

"Yes." She wavered a little on her feet and backed up a step.

"What about my lips?" He followed her.

Pink flushed her cheeks and her eyes grew bright. "Y-yes. You're killing me here."

"Oh, if my fingers and my lips cause you problems, do you mind teeth?" He skimmed his touch down to trace the outer curve of one breast. The nipple puckered beautifully and poked at the fabric. His body hummed with the need to caress, to shape, to pinch, to twist, and play with her until those soft hitching breaths were all she was capable of. "What if I want to scrape my teeth lightly over that very pointed nipple and suck on it?"

Her fingers curled into his shirt and she tugged him forward, the fire in her eyes incandescent. "Are you going to talk me into an orgasm, Richard? Or actually put your hands where your mouth seems intent on going?"

"I thought you'd never ask," he teased just to watch her eyes widen and her temper flare. *Gotcha.* Snaking an arm around her waist, he bent and took her legs out from under her and swung her up into his arms. "Hold on and, if your shoulder twinges, you tell me."

It wasn't a request.

Her lashes swept down and when they came up again, mischief grew in her smile. "Yes, sir. Thank you, sir." The reminder of his boast about seducing his secretary amused him.

Pinching her ass in retaliation, he laughed. "Armand should never have told you that story."

"I'm glad he did." She took advantage of their position to tug down the collar of his shirt and pressed her lips to the flesh she revealed. Flames kindled in his blood and he picked up the pace, saving any words for the top of the stairs.

"Why are you so glad he did?" It took him a minute to remember which room was his. Hell, they all were and they all had beds, but he wanted her in his room and in *his* bed.

"He loves you, very much." Her answer surprised him and he paused just inside the door of his room to meet her gaze. "It's a rare thing to see men being openly affectionate about their relationships, but you mean the world to him. I think it was his way of telling me that I shouldn't take advantage of you."

Grappling with that idea for a moment, he carried her to the bed and sat down, cradling her in his lap. Nuzzling her forehead and then her cheek, he murmured, "I think it was his way of messing with me."

"Has it occurred to you that he managed to do both in one simple statement?" She traced the line of his jaw, pressing a row of sweet, butterfly kisses all the way to his throat and he lifted his head, letting her play. The feel of her bottom pressed against his lap and the weight of her on his chest was an erotic sensation he wouldn't trade for anything.

"With him, anything is possible," he mused. Armand had surprised him over the years with his choices and the lengths to which he would go. "However, if you have any other comments about him, let's get those out of the way right now."

She glanced at him, brows raised in lazy question.

"No more questions? Comments? General statements where Armand is concerned?"

"It's so tempting to tease you right now, considering how incredibly tight my body is wound and how much I want to strip off your clothes and feel you thrusting inside of me..."

Galvanized by her words, he leaned away enough to lift the hem of her shirt and she helped him pull it off. She tapped his own impatiently, but he ignored the request, his attention locked on the beautiful curves he'd just revealed. While not petite, her breasts more than filled his hands and were capped by the dark, puckered rosettes. "Dark cherries in sweet cream," he whispered and swung her down onto the bed easily—careful, always careful, of her shoulder.

The hungry, aching need inside him enthusiastic in its demand. It didn't want to play anymore, it wanted to touch and to taste and to savor. A dozen different erotic images danced through his mind and he cupped one breast and gave in to the urge to stroke his thumb across the peak. Capturing her gasp in a hot, languorous kiss, the rational part of his brain shut off and he abandoned her mouth with a nip to her lower lip then dipped to pull one plumped nipple between his teeth.

Her fingers fisted in his hair and she arched her back. A hiss dragged his head up and he glared at her. "You have to lay still, no pain for you."

"No." Defiance roiled in the word. "Stop talking and kiss me."

"Yes, ma'am." He kissed her hard and slid a hand down to undo her shorts. Nibbling a path back to her abandoned breast, he closed his teeth around the nipple and slid his hand into her shorts. Her gasps turned to a whimper and he divided his attention between licking and sucking each breast and teasing his fingers into the damp folds between her thighs.

Nothing with Kate was halfway. She thrust her hands into his hair, pulling him impatiently closer. Her thighs spread and her hips arched to each teasing caress of his finger. He pressed the heel of his hand against her clit and the muscles of her neck went taut. Lifting his head from her breast, he watched the orgasm roll over her as he teased it from her.

It was the most erotic sight he'd ever seen.

Slipping his hand free, he rose enough to tug her shorts down and the scrap of lace panties. Holding them up, he stared at her with a grin. His very put-together, professional Kate liked lace. He would drown her in it. Sprawled against the dark coverlet, she gave him a smile filled with lazy pleasure. "You have too many clothes on."

"I'm working on that." But he wasn't. He wanted to drink in his fill of her beauty. Of her supple, taut curves, the shape of her hip and the sweet, sweep of her legs. So much strength housed in one extremely feminine body.

Lifting her right leg, he pressed a kiss against her calf then again to the inside of her knee then again to her thigh. She tracked his progress, curled her leg, rubbing her foot against his back.

Slipping his hands under bottom, he teased the soft skin with his thumbs and dipped down to lick her once from her slick entrance to her clit. "You didn't let me mention this part downstairs." He had no idea where he found the words, but he wanted to tell her everything. He wanted her as engaged in every part of his discovery of her.

"Oh?" Strain added a higher note to her voice and he smiled, nuzzling a kiss against her pussy and then spearing his tongue inside. Her hips bucked and he teased her with a series of bites and licks.

But he saved the best for last, locking his mouth around the tight bundle of nerves and drawing on it, "hmmm." And she came again, in a wild explosion. Her thighs clamped against his shoulders and he held on, drawing out the pleasure until she shook from it.

Lifting his head, he gazed at her until she managed to open her eyes and look at him again. "Oh yes, I want to do that a few more times, but someone was very ready." He dragged a finger through the slick folds, the damp scent of her arousal like a drug he could very easily become addicted to.

"I blame you, utterly." Even drunk on passion she still managed to sass him.

"What can I do to make it up to you?" He eased a finger inside her and her eyes darkened, but she never looked away.

"Hmm. Lukewarm." But the perspiration dotting her skin and the ragged quality of her breathing made that a lie.

"Hmm, how is this?" He slid in a second finger, testing her tightness and her hips arched.

"Warmer." But she wasn't done playing and the muscles in her throat stood out in stark relief.

"I guess you need something more?" He worked his fingers in and out, a gentle thrusting motion and her lips parted.

"More...would...b-be—better." The broken quality of speech told him more than anything else just how ready she was. Giving her clit another soft kiss, he eased his fingers out then stood. Shedding his clothes quickly, he pulled a condom out of the drawer next to the bed.

She stared, openly studying his body and he resisted the urge to puff out his chest. His cock ached with so much need it bordered on painful. Rolling the condom on, he barely noticed the shaking in his hands.

"That's—definitely more." This time, her words held a provocative invitation and he grinned.

"So you'll let me know if I get to hot?" He couldn't wait until her shoulder was healed. They could *really* play then.

"C'mere," she whispered and held out her arms. Unwilling and unable to deny her anything, he settled back into the cradle of her thighs and braced his weight on his arms. He didn't want to hurt her.

But instead of lying still, she wrapped her arms around his neck and dug her nails into his back. "I'm not that fragile, Richard." The rebuke was both passionate and serious.

Easing forward, he teased both of them, rocking his erection against her. Her legs wrapped around his hips and she dragged his head down for an impatient kiss. He shifted his lower body and her thighs clamped against him.

Breaking the kiss, he reached between them and nudged inside her an inch. She'd been so damn tight while he played and he didn't want to—

Kate's legs crossed behind him and she anchored him, arching her hips and locking him down at the same moment. He slid into her all the way to the hilt.

The overload damn near had his eyes crossing.

Fisting his hand into the covers, he tried to glare at her, but she caught his face in her hands and whispered, "Move."

The last rational link in his restraint snapped and the only thoughts he had were how exquisite she looked and felt, pulsing around him as he rocked into her. She stroked his shoulders, her nails biting into his flesh. Her mouth opened and he wasn't sure who claimed who, because she became everything. The world crashed around him in a wild tidal wave of lust, and need, and something far more indefinable that a part of his heart recognized as love. Then there was nothing but Kate and he came with a surge that left him shaken to the core.

~

SOMETIME DURING THE EVENING, he woke to the feel of her mouth on him. The slow, sensuous torture turned into the longest—and definitely the second most erotic—experience in his life. By the time she'd wrenched every drop of an orgasm from him and snuggled back into his arms, he thought he could die happy. Waking to her sound asleep against his chest, her hair spread out against him and her leg nestled securely between his filled him with a very rare contentment.

The buzz of his cell phone intruded and he stretched to grab it, careful not to wake Kate. George's Pizza flashed on the caller ID and he answered immediately.

They didn't call on the weekend if they could help.

"What's wrong? Is everything all right?"

"She's ready to talk, but I don't know if she'll stay that way." Diane Fowler's response was blunt and on point. "Can you come out to see her today?"

"I can try." He frowned. It would be harder to elude Armand's security during the day. Tracing his fingers along Kate's spine, he considered his options. "I'll be there later tonight. I'll call when I'm on my way."

"Thank you, you made an impression yesterday. She's just scared."

"I know," he murmured, his voice still low. "It will be fine, I'll be with you as soon as I can."

Diane said her goodbyes and the call disconnected with a soft click. After returning the cell phone to the nightstand, he smiled at the morning sunlight playing across his ceiling. Apparently they'd never gotten around to closing his curtains. Not that he cared. Kate ran her palm up his side and he heard her yawn before she lifted her head. "Good morning."

"Good morning."

"Who was on the phone?" She smothered a yawn.

"Nobody." No one she needed to know about anyway. He could so get used to sleepy, soft, doe-eyed Kate. Indulging his pleasure at finding her plastered against him, he ran an exploratory hand over her hip

"Hmm, you do wake up chipper. I was afraid of that." Her eyes closed and she pressed her ear to his chest. His heart thumped hard against his ribs.

"Nothing wrong with being a morning person," he chided her. Not that he really was, but waking up to Kate in his arms? That gave a man a reason to be happy.

"Hmm," came her grunt of a response.

"Oh." Surprise filtered through his enjoyment. "You aren't a morning person?"

Another grunt. She petted him. "More sleep."

Pleased by the wonderful new insight, he rolled her over and nuzzled the corner of her mouth. "You go ahead and sleep," he murmured and began another lazy exploration of her neck and dipped lower. "You might lay still this time for me to play."

But she didn't.

And he really didn't mind.

It took them another two hours before they managed to roll out of bed, then they broke more rules in the shower. Fortunately, he'd gotten a good look at her stitches and the shoulder actually looked better rather than worse, though the bruise managed to be uglier. Still, he'd been pretty aggressive with her the night before and she'd not been remotely shy about returning the attention. Some wounds hurt worse a couple of days later.

"I told you I was fine." She watched him over the rim of her coffee cup.

"I know, but I also know you have a legendary pain tolerance and I wanted to make sure you weren't sore from last night." He on the other hand, ached beautifully and had the scratches on his back to prove it. The look on her face had been priceless when she'd spotted them. When he'd teased her about going out to pick up the mail sans his shirt, she'd actually looked so mortified he'd left it alone.

"Oh, I'm sore." She shifted in the chair and reached for the Sunday paper. "But in all the right ways."

Smug, he tugged out the business section and let her have the rest. "Good. Anything you want to do today?"

"I already did who I wanted to do today."

Glancing up from the paper he met her wicked smile and waggled his brows. "Well I hope you don't mind when he wants to do you again."

"I'm impressed by your commitment to stamina."

Laughing, he reached for his coffee cup. "When your woman is as physically fit as you are, a man has to do what a man has to do."

Shifting forward, Kate put a hand on his arm. "I like what you can do."

Catching her hand, he lifted it to kiss her fingertips. "Ditto, sweetheart. Ditto." He watched her a moment longer as she curled back into her chair, one leg crossed over the other and the news section opened. She didn't go for the lifestyle, but he did see the comics next in her stack and grinned to himself.

He could definitely get used to this.

They spent a leisurely morning on the deck, enjoying the sunshine and the paper. Occasionally she showed him an article she found interesting and they debated the editorials. He conned her into another round of *Call of Duty* after lunch and she fell asleep against him on the sofa an hour after dinner in the middle of *A Few Good Men*.

Content, he let her sleep and roused her only enough to get her up to bed. His bed. With regret, he tucked her in and slipped out quietly. This late, the house was dark and he knew where Armand's security was. He avoided them on his way around the house and then down a series of steps till he reached the beach. The moonless night was the perfect cover.

Four hours later, he crept back into the house the way he had gone out.

Exhausted, he stripped and slid into bed. He didn't want to wake her, but when he went to sleep, it was spooned up against her back.

～

MONDAY ARRIVED with a fresh dose of reality. "So." Kate poured coffee for both of them. She'd been quiet in the shower, quieter still why they dressed.

"Chickening out?" he asked quietly, aware of the distance she'd already put between them.

"No." She wrinkled her nose and held out a mug to him. "Just working out how we'll do this."

"Which part? I thought what we did in the shower worked really well." He couldn't help but tease her. He didn't like the cool, professional wall she'd begun erecting after she came apart in his arms all slick, wet and soapy.

She paused, coffee cup halfway to her lips. "I do believe you were more than adequate. However, I was referring to your morning schedule."

"Adequate?" he repeated. "Adequate?"

The corner of her mouth twitched. "It's after eight, Richard. Do focus. We're on the clock which means it's my job to keep you on time. I can stroke your ego later."

Hardly mollified, he gave her a dirty look. "Adequate." He'd show her adequate.

"Focus." She walked over to the table and flipped on her digital tablet. "You have four conference calls scheduled this morning, one starting in about thirty minutes. Do you want to take it here? Or in the car? Or would you like me to reschedule it? Unless something changed last night when you went out."

The last sentence echoed with a question, but he focused on the first part instead. "The call in thirty minutes is Kravitts, isn't it?" Grimacing, he pushed away his irritation at her businesslike tone. They did have work to do and she was his assistant.

"Yes, it's regarding the Masterson deal he's trying to curry with the EU. What he wants is for you to represent the corporate interests and provide second chair support to his in-house counsel when they present their deal to the commission in Belgium next month." The succinct summary covered most aspects of what Kravitts had scheduled the call for.

"I can't represent their interests. It would be a direct conflict with the *Spherecast* deal."

"A conflict of interest he wants to put you in. It's most likely a fishing expedition to see if you'll tell him no so he can pursue why. It also allows him to play the 'in negotiations with Andraste Enterprises' card." Since he'd said the same thing a couple of weeks ago, he had to grin.

"So why did I agree to the call?" He dared her to remember because he'd only told her to set it up. He hadn't said why.

"To mollify him while you finished negotiating for Mr. Voldakov and His Highness." She tapped her nail against the side of the tablet. "Which means you can cancel this call because it's already served its purpose simply by being on the books."

"That would be a calculated and cold move on my part." He sipped his coffee.

"How much notice of the cancellation would you like me to give him?" Understanding lit her eyes.

Moments like this reminded him exactly how much he adored her mind. "Two minutes."

"You are a mean man, Mr. Prentiss." But she checked her phone for a time and marked out the call on the tablet. "You have a call thirty minutes after that with His Highness and Mr. Voldakov. They've both confirmed their availability. Mr. Grange, Mr. Voldakov's attorney, will be placing the call. Do you want to take that one in the office?"

"I think I should take that one naked while you're sitting in my lap." He stared at her across the table. Rattling her in the office would be a hell of a lot of fun, but once they were there, he'd need to behave. It was one thing to tease her across a breakfast table, something else entirely where he met with his clients.

Of course, the idea of going down on her while she sprawled across his desk held a great deal of appeal.

"I hardly think nudity will be conducive to a successfully negotiated business arrangement." Her face flushed and her tongue skated over her lip. Recognizing the signs of her arousal, he stroked his finger around the rim of his coffee cup.

"It's a done deal, Kate. This is the notification call and I won't have to do any talking at all. Imagine listening to all that formal protocol as Daniel and Armand dance around their family connection and Martin has to play negotiator while I slide in and out of you. They're all tense and proper with their blood pressure on the rise and your legs are wrapped around my waist and we're having a good time."

She set the tablet down with a thump. The rapidly escalating rise and fall of her chest betrayed her. "You do not fight fair."

"No, I don't, but you keep thinking about that 'adequate' time I gave you while I take this call in my office." He rose and drained his coffee cup. Leaving it on the counter, he pivoted to give her a wink. "Be sure to sit in. I wouldn't want you to miss a *moment* of it."

The dishtowel caught him in the back of his head as he walked away.

His good mood lasted all the way out to the car and even having to let Armand's security give them a ride to the office, he still managed to enjoy himself.

She retaliated, however, by sucking on a pen the whole ride and pretending interest in whatever she read on the tablet.

No, being with Kate would never be boring.

CHAPTER 12
KATE

The ease with which they fell into a routine surprised Kate—the fact that she let him get away with lying to her surprised her more. Nights and weekends were spent at his house. They'd stopped at her apartment to pack up two full suitcases so she had plenty of clothes. But on two separate occasions, she'd found him gone and his security completely unaware that he'd left. She'd suspected it that first weekend, but when it happened twice in the same week and he gave her no explanation she couldn't excuse it or brush it off.

The fact that he'd done it on her watch added to the sting.

First in the office that morning, and then again *after* they'd gone home. He'd mentioned reviewing some contracts and that he'd join her in the pool, but he was a no show. She'd searched the whole house and he wasn't present.

His security was still on the gate. Giving in to temptation, she turned on the GPS tracker in his

215

phone and found it—in his home office. He'd left it sitting right on the desk. Picking it up, Kate turned the device over in her hand.

Since meeting Richard, she'd never seen him without his phone. Panic burned like a flash fire in her system.

If he left it here... The door creaked behind her and she turned. Richard stood in the entryway, keys in one hand and his expression unreadable. "Hey."

"Hey?" Irritation scraped along the inside of her skin. Holding up his phone, she raised her brows. "Where did you go?"

He flicked a look from her to the phone, then back to her. "I thought we might grill by the pool for dinner." That wasn't an answer. He set the keys down on the bookshelf and shrugged out of the suit coat—a different one from what he'd worn to the office.

"Richard?"

"Or we can order in." He gave her an easy smile. "Whatever you want. Though, I like the second option because it means we can eat in bed. What do you fancy? Chinese? Thai? Mediterranean?"

Kate grew tired of biting her tongue. It hurt. "I'll pick up something on my way back to my apartment." She tossed his phone and strode past while he fumbled to catch it.

"Hey." Richard followed her down the hall and then up the stairs. But she didn't stop, and continued to the guest room where she'd left her overnight bags. Her shoulder throbbed with the tension cramping her muscles, however, she continued moving. If she stopped she'd either cry or punch him.

She didn't really feel like doing either.

Richard's hand came down on her arm and stopped her at the door. "Kate, stop."

After halting, she refused to turn. "Yes?"

"You're angry." And his almost conciliatory tone was the last straw.

"No, I want to shower, change and go to my apartment." Firming her lips into a thin line, she pivoted to face him. Since he'd ducked answering her question without any pretense of lying, she waited a beat.

He sighed. "Look, Kate, you're mad because I left, but I had somewhere I needed to be."

Which wasn't really an answer. Her pulse thrummed with the surge of adrenaline. He'd been out there, alone and exposed. Anything could have happened. "You're an idiot." She shoved him back a step, then retreated into the guest room and slammed the door in his face for good measure.

Fuming, she scanned the room for her bags. They'd been on the bed and now they weren't. Crossing the bedroom to the closet, she pulled it open. All of the new clothes with their tags still in place seemed to mock her, she still had no idea why he had the clothes. Unfortunately, her bags weren't in evidence. Aggravated, she headed back to the door.

One part of her mind seemed to take a step back, and recognized her wholly irrational reaction as that of a jealous, worried lover instead of the cool practicality that came from being a bodyguard.

But I am his damn lover. She'd given up the bodyguard gig and traded it in for his bed. Fists clenched, she stopped just short of the door. His leaving without word or security baffled her on all levels—the soldier and the woman. Blowing up didn't help her cause. Exhaling a long breath, she tried to gather up the ragged ends of her temper.

Opening the door to his cool, impersonal attorney's face aggravated her all over again.

"As I was saying," he began as though she'd never slammed the door. "I had somewhere I needed to be—"

She cut him off with a wave of her hand. "Without your security?"

"Look, if they can't figure out how I'm getting out then neither can the people they're supposed to be protecting me from. And I still think that was a random act of violence and the only reason I haven't called Armand on his over protectiveness is that *you* were hurt." Anger tensed his jaw and for a moment, she saw the same flash of danger in him she'd seen that day on the golf course when he'd taken on Bing in her defense.

The flutter in her stomach warned her she found it just as attractive now as she had then. That only served to piss her off more. "I can't believe you would endanger yourself so recklessly."

Impatience mixed with arrogance cooled his dark eyes. "You let me worry about the choices I make. Now, did you have a preference about dinner?"

Frost hung off his every word and she nearly shivered, suddenly aware that she wore only her bathing suit with a towel wrapped around her waist. "So you're done discussing this?"

"Yes, I am. I'm sorry you're upset," he said, cool dismissal in each syllable. "But you were safe here and that's what mattered. And like I said, it's not my problem the so-called bodyguards can't figure out how I'm leaving..." Whatever else he said faded as her temper spiked.

He was absolutely right. It wasn't their fault they didn't know how he did it. She hadn't reported his absences. With that thought riding her, she spun away from him again and headed for the stairs.

"Kate?"

She ignored him for the second time in as many minutes and took the stairs two at a time. Her shoulder still ached, but it had nothing on the sick feeling in her stomach. If Richard got himself killed on her watch... She couldn't complete that thought.

It mattered to her.

He mattered.

In his office, she picked up the keys and looked at them. There were three—and one was for a vehicle. She ducked around him and checked the garage, neither of the cars responded to it. When he went to block her path, she eluded him again.

"What the hell are you doing?" he demanded

and followed her as she went out the back door to the deck and the pool. No way he left via the front with the guards. They would know. So that left somewhere from the deck—which meant he'd slipped out either while she was swimming laps or while she'd changed.

The deck overlooked the beach, and the rock face was pretty sheer, but that didn't mean it was *all* sheer.

"Kate," Richard repeated, standing at her elbow now. "What are you doing?"

"Figuring out how you do it." She told him bluntly. "If you want to endanger yourself, then I need to know not only when, but how." If that meant following him next time she would.

Scrubbing a hand over his face, Richard eyed her. "You don't have to do that."

Oh the hell I don't. But she kept that sentiment to herself as she studied the lay of the land.

The pool area was gated, and boasted a significant fence, not that it needed one—nothing about it was visible from the road or the beach and his nearest neighbor was more than a half mile away.

Prowling past him, she walked the perimeter and if she hadn't been looking for it, she wouldn't have seen the difference in the boards.

A gate blended into the fence line—it had no actual handle, just a different seam for the wood. Across the pool, nestled against the rocks was another more obvious gate, but those were for the pool cleaner and pump. Richard stopped a pace behind her and she glanced at him once, then pushed the slightly off-sized wooden panel and heard the distinct pop and lock as the gate opened.

The sun slid down the western sky, but there was still plenty of light to see the slightly worn track that led from the gate over the hill. She made it three steps before Richard said, "Wait—please."

The trail was nestled right against the hill. She couldn't see the road or the beach. The house blocked it from view. "Are you going to tell me now?"

"Kate, you have bare feet."

That wasn't an answer, so she plunged onward intent on following the trail.

"For the love of God, you're stubborn." He all but growled the words. Aww, had she pissed him off?

Good.

"I'm sorry pot, what did you call the kettle?" But her temper had cooled, because she could see the trail went for a ways and if it continued down the side of the hill, it likely let out in one of the other neighborhoods.

She glanced at the keys in her hand. It wouldn't be hard to park a car there or rent a garage.

"Stop. Seriously, stop." Richard caught up to her. When he took her arm and tugged her around, she let him. Worry furrowed his brow. "If you don't know the way, you could get hurt."

"I'm a big girl. I can take care of myself, remember?" But it wasn't his words that halted her but the bleak expression on his face.

"I remember you getting shot because you were with me," he said quietly. "Come back inside. *Trust* me." When she didn't move immediately, he cupped her chin and brought his forehead to hers. "I promise the next time I go, I'll tell you."

"Take me with you," she countered.

"Kate..."

"No, if I'm in, I'm in." God, was she in. Losing him would be harder than losing a limb. She'd been stupid not to realize how far she'd fallen for him. "Let me in."

He sighed. "Babe, don't you understand how far you already are?"

She was a damn hypocrite, being angry with him for keeping secrets when she had yet to share her own, but he'd— "You scared me," she admitted aloud even as the thought occurred to her. "When I realized you were out without anyone protecting you."

The last trace of remoteness left his expression and when he drew her into his arms, she went. "And for that, I'm sorry," he whispered it against her lips and then kissed her.

Yeah, she was gone, because she let him lead her back inside. They didn't discuss where he went, and upstairs she found that he'd transferred her clothes into his closet.

She was so screwed.

A part of her knew she had to tell the security force about the back exit, but the rest of her wanted to protect his secret—his freedom. But she wouldn't let him go alone next time. And there would be a next time, of that she had no doubt. She wanted—no she needed to know where he was going.

~

THE NEXT WEEK passed with an almost uneasy truce, she found herself second guessing everything he told her and more than once, she caught him studying her with the same look of consternation.

They rode together to the office, more often than not in her car because he had calls. If he needed her on the call, he let security drive them. The grand duke's security force took up a greater presence in their lives. Not only did they man the gate at Richard's house, but she encouraged the assignment of a man to their floor at the office, and to reception. A visible deterrent to future attempts. It also discouraged Richard from leaving the office undetected, though she'd discovered his private elevator and access on the other side of his bathroom. It was an express elevator that went to the garage. How he'd managed that, she had no idea—but she knew damn good and well they weren't on the plans his personal security force had.

Working with Richard continued to entertain her, even though their relationship seemed punctuated with strain and tension. It had been a long seven days since the night she caught him coming back—and to her knowledge, he hadn't slipped away again—when he stopped at her desk, his expression sober and intense. "Kate, cancel all our plans for tonight."

"All right—what's up?"

"Just be ready to go at seven. I'm going to show you where I go." After that announcement, he'd shut himself up for the rest of the day on writing a brief.

By evening she was wired. He drove, and she was aware of the security follow cars—more surprised that Richard didn't even try to evade.

Guilt stabbed at her. "Are you sure you want me here?"

"Yes." No hesitation marked his response. He parked in the driveway of a North Hollywood home on a cracked street called Bonner Avenue. It looked like any of the other houses on the block, a little larger, a little less kempt with a yard full of toys, but it was clean and in good repair. Twisting in his seat, he gave her a long look. "Do you remember what I told you about the Christine Center?"

The place his mother had taken him and his sister after his father's arrests. *Oh shit. He said one of the center's benefactors thought enough of his mother to send her back to school to get a degree and hired her...* "Yes."

"This is one of their outreaches. Currently it's home to about a dozen displaced mothers and their children as well as four staff members and three part time counselors." He turned off the car. "Behind the main house, they have some acreage and a smaller house that doubles as an office and counseling center. On those nights that I 'disappear'—I come here."

"Oh, hell." No wonder he didn't say anything about where he went. The clothes. Richard had benefitted from Christine's Center and, in return, he'd grown up to be one of its benefactors. Five bedrooms in the house and he lived alone, but that guest bedroom had a number of clothes in the closet and they were all brand new, tags still on them. "You rescue them. You bring them back to your place." The secret exits from his office and his house.

Richard gave her a faint smile. "Sometimes they need a fast exit, a safe one."

Her heart squeezed and it took her a minute to get her emotions back under control. Once out of the car, Richard led her down the driveway. Behind them, the security car pulled out and headed down the road. Kate stopped and stared after it. "Richard?"

"I told them they couldn't stay here." He paused, cupping her elbow. "This is a quiet place for these women to get their lives back under their control. They accept me here because I am one of them and I'm also an attorney and I help them get their lives back. Those guys are big, hulking brutes with guns and they don't need the intimidation."

"And you were going to mention the lack of security when?" Worry tipped through her. She let him walk her up the driveway, better to be far away from the street. The quiet residential area didn't hold any elements of menace, but that sure as hell didn't mean they weren't there.

How many cars had been on the street? She hadn't been paying attention, not when Richard had been driving and she'd been trying to reconcile her own guilt and anger.

"It's fine." He nudged open the gate. "They've been everywhere the last month or so and it's been quiet. I think we really were caught in a random crapstorm that day. Don't worry." He dropped a kiss on her lips. "I'll text them when we're ready to go."

Trusting that they wouldn't go far was about the best she could do. Peterson's guys knew Richard's habits.

They also knew the threat against the Andraste family better than anyone.

No one could get close to the family—Richard made an easier and far more attractive target considering his close personal ties to the prince. A man they'd dined with three times in as many weeks.

And there was nothing uncomfortable about that...

Blowing out a breath, she calmed her erratic heart. Fortunately, her research into his cases at the firm hadn't flagged any threats—but then she hadn't had access to his cases for the Center. Kate grimaced, glad for the darkness that hid her expression. Richard wasn't alone, not when she had his back.

Inside, she identified three benefits to the building. First, the location behind the main house meant no direct line of sight existed to the street. Second, the room Richard took his meetings in was located in the back of the building with a single window that faced a brick wall. Third, and best of all, the four women sitting in a group waiting for him weren't armed and cheered up immensely at his arrival.

They were wary of her, but Kate didn't mind. She tried to relax her shoulders and appear as nonthreatening as possible, but they didn't know her and they weren't prepared to trust her. She accepted that judgment without comment.

Richard introduced her to the first client, Valerie Manning—she and her four sons were all residents at Christine's Center. She'd lost her job as a high school teacher after filing for an injunction against her abusive ex-husband. Richard handled a pair of cases for her—the first against the district for wrongful termination and the second against her ex-husband to terminate his parental rights.

By the time that meeting ended, Valerie was in tears and gave him a hug. Kate stared at the closed door, then at him. He'd never raised his voice or been anything more than solicitous, yet she could feel the quiet rage behind his professional veneer.

"What's going to happen to the douche ex-husband?" She had the unreasonable urge to deliver a cease-and-desist order with a baseball bat and she didn't know Valerie.

"He's cooling his heels in jail right now. He violated the restraining order last month and trespassed." Despite his matter-of-fact tone, he smiled tightly. "He might have had an open container in his vehicle and taken a swing at the officer who came to arrest him too. We have another thirty days and I'll have Mrs. Manning relocated by then." Richard filled out the last of the paperwork and handed it over to her. "We'll need to file those first thing in the morning. Exigent orders for emergency temporary custody so she can move across a state line. Did she sign the power of attorney so I can handle the rest of it?"

She nodded. Valerie hadn't hesitated when Richard told her about the job waiting for her in Arizona and the rental house that had been "donated" for her use for a few months. If Kate hadn't already been falling in love with him, his care and dedication to these women would have sealed the deal. Clearing her throat, she paused next to him and brushed the hair away from his forehead. "Ready for the next one?"

"Yes." He shot her a quick smile and tucked the first file away into his bag and pulled out the next. "Kathy Sanderson."

Each case seemed to be bad on its own merits. One woman had lost everything to a house fire and the insurance company refused to pay. They had to go over her deposition preparation for the following week. Another had been arrested for possession of a controlled substance—she'd had a bottle of oxy in her purse that she'd taken from a coworker to help them stay clean—and now her three-year-old daughter was in CPS custody. Richard held her when she cried because he'd gotten the mother a visitation order and a judge would hear her case within the month about restoring her custodianship if she promised to complete drug rehabilitation offered by the center.

The last case got to Kate.

Really got her.

Side-swiped by a drunk driver, Melissa Kent had suffered a traumatic brain injury. According to the files, prior to the accident Kent had been a successful attorney with a promising career. After it, she struggled to remember where her office was located much less the legal code. Her husband had left her and taken custody of the children. She couldn't hold down a job longer than a few days before she began to forget what she was supposed to do.

The accident left her with a seven-day window of time to start again and again and again. Richard took the time to reintroduce himself, explained the case, their progress, and that the other driver's insurance company and hers had agreed to mediation. Melissa would not only receive the medical care she needed, the money would be available to see to her care for years to come and help her children.

It had to be hell. Kate's eyes were damp as the woman shuffled out. One of the others had waited for her and escorted her back up to the main house.

"Hey..." Richard wrapped an arm around her middle and pulled her back against him. "Are you crying?"

"No," she lied and blinked the tears. "How do you do that?"

"One case a time, Kate." Comfort. God, he offered her comfort and he did this all the time. "One case at a time. I'm helping them the only way I can." He nuzzled the side of her head. "And you helped them too."

"How?" She turned to look at him. "I handed you files and called names."

"You didn't judge them." The intensity in his gaze held her captive. "You stood there, quiet, composed and strong. Did you watch them watching you? They'd talk about their case or listen to me when I did but they'd glance at you. When Valerie asked me what she should do about that emergency order and her ex-husband, you lifted your chin and you looked fierce. I could see it in your body language—you wanted to kick his ass."

Heat flushed her face. "I don't like jerks who beat their wives and she got a raw deal."

"Yes, she did. But she was afraid of you when she came in. She wasn't when she left because you were on her side." Was that pride in his voice? "Maybe it's only a little thing, but those women saw another strong woman in here, a woman who is helping them face the crap life threw at them, and that tells them that maybe they can do it too. So, yeah, you helped. A lot." He pressed his lips to hers and she savored the sweetness in his kiss.

"You're amazing." She licked her lips and shook her head as she stepped back.

He winked. "In a totally adequate way, right?"

"Oh, I think you passed adequate and moved right on to better than expected." His laughter washed over her and she double-checked the files to make sure he had his and she had the right ones to carry to the courthouse. "Hungry?"

"Starving." He checked behind the table before pushing all the chairs in. "I say we stop at some all-night fast-food place and grab some burgers, take them home, and eat them naked."

The salacious offer stroked over the raw edges left from their series of meetings and she led the way out into the waiting area and opened the exterior door. True night had fallen and it was pitch black outside save for the pools of light cast from the front house. "I don't think I'm in the mood for burgers. What do you think of Chinese or—ooh, how about some Thai?"

"So we pick up some Thai and take it home and eat it naked." He didn't miss a beat. Kate was still laughing as she pivoted to face him.

It gave her a front row view to all the blood draining from his face.

The gun pressed against the back of her head froze her in place and all traces of humor vanished. Richard's gaze locked with hers and she could see the fear a heartbeat before it calmed and his attention went to the person with the gun. "Let her leave. She's not a part of this."

"But she's important to you, Mr. Prentiss." *A man.* His voice was rough, a little nasal and a hell of a lot angry. With the steel barrel flush against her scalp, she didn't dare move.

Security car is on the street... And the panic button was in her pocket attached to her keys. She'd transferred them from her purse to her jacket pocket when they were setting up for their meetings. If she could reach them, she might be able to set the button off without getting a bullet in the head for her trouble.

"She's my assistant." Richard's tone turned chill. "They're hard to find."

"That you just want to eat food with naked, sure. You like expensive things, living in your expensive house and, hell, this is a pretty lady. I'm sure she's pretty pricey too." Something was off about the man's voice—the taunts. It didn't fit the profile of one of the fanatics trying to off the royal family.

They were after political capital and big, splashy statements.

A man with a gun in the dark? That said personal.

Too personal.

Time to redirect his attention. "What do you want?"

Richard's gaze lasered on her. She saw the order in them and ignored it. He wanted her to be quiet, to let him handle it. No. Being quiet allowed the gunman to focus on Richard. That could get him shot.

Unacceptable.

"Do you know who he is?" The gunman eased closer to her. A miasma of tobacco, smoke and astringent surrounded her. Based on body heat, he had to be within inches of her body, but only the gun touched her head and it didn't move.

"Clearly she knows who I am." Richard attempted to regain his attention. "She works for me."

"No, she works for hotshot attorney Richard Prentiss, pretty boy front man for big name corporations and royal families, but does she know you're a fraud? That's what I want to know." A whine interjected into the nasal snarl of his voice, a break in his speech patterns suggesting that his education hadn't continued much past high school. He pressed the gun into her head with more force and she looked down.

She dropped the files in her left hand and reached for her right pocket at the same time. His feet were visible behind her. He couldn't be more than three or four inches behind her. Easily in jabbing range.

"Do. You. Know. Who. He. Is? Did he tell you about how he got his money? How his Daddy took it? How he rubs elbows with the rich and the famous and my family got nothing?" Anger coated in desperation. Definitely personal. He didn't want to make a statement.

He wanted revenge.

Richard let out a long breath because he'd gotten it too. She spared him a look. The shadows around his eyes hid his emotions well, but she knew it had to hurt. He hated what his father had done. "Look, what's your name?" He'd gone from deal making to placating—a guy like this wouldn't respond to either. He wanted to hurt someone and he'd picked Richard to hurt.

Fingering her pocket, she found the panic button and pressed it.

"Yeah, you don't know my name. Why should you? I'm just some chump whose family your father screwed." Rage made his tone nastier. "You like getting where you have by walking on other people? You think it makes you untouchable?" A hard hand locked on her neck, but the palm was slippery with sweat and the pain only sharpened her focus and gave her a window because he'd moved his gun. The man holding her couldn't be quite six feet and he had strength in his grip, but he was nervous and the hand with the gun trembled. "You make all the right noises and send checks off to charity, all the while keeping your pockets lined with the money of other hard-up people. Just like your father."

"He's nothing like his father," Kate interjected. *Pay attention to me. Pay attention to me.*

"Kate, shush," Richard ordered, then switched rolls to negotiator. "My father is a son of a bitch who stole from people. He took their money and he buried it. I have no idea what he did with it or where it went. I never saw a penny, but if you want a check today for the full amount, I'll write you one. Just let her go. No one has to get hurt. Too many people have already been hurt."

"Yeah, well, if you'd just died in your car, this would have been over and the pretty lady wouldn't be in the middle of it." Spittle flew out with the words and his hand trembled more.

Where the hell are they? It had only been seconds—some rational part of her mind recognized that fact. But when a man had a gun, seconds counted.

"Fine, you want to shoot me?" Richard spread his arms wide. "I'm right here. Shoot me. But you let her go first. She had nothing to do with this or with my father. This is you and me."

Kate's heart stopped again. Was he insane?

He just told the crazy man with the gun to shoot him.

The fingers biting into her neck jerked her back one step and she took it, slamming her heel down on the man's foot and driving her arm up hard to knock his aim toward the ceiling.

The world slowed down. Kate kept moving. All she had to do was lock the guy's arm up. A pressure point in his elbow would make him release the gun. But Richard lunged forward and the man's rage bounced off the walls around them. A glancing punch caught her in the ear and he brought the gun down, pointed directly at Richard.

At this distance, he couldn't miss. She wrenched back from the struggle and stepped right into the path. The bullet slammed into her chest, then a second one burned a path through her abdomen. The force struck like two sledgehammer blows and she exhaled hard.

Another shot cracked through the silence and fear clawed at her. She didn't feel that bullet.

Richard! But it was the gunman who dropped and Kate shuddered, staring across the floor at the man's bloodied forehead.

A single bullet hole marred the side of his temple—the other side of his head was gone.

Noise imploded into the room on the rush of feet and then Richard was over her shouting. He had his hands pressed against her chest but she couldn't make out the words.

Fuck that hurts.

Hurt worse, ten times worse, than her shoulder popping out of the socket. A hundred times worse than the bullet grazing her a month before.

Still, so much better than Richard being shot.

"Hurt?" she managed to spit the word out on a bubble of blood. She couldn't breathe and it made it impossible to talk.

"Help is coming. You stay with me," he ordered. "Dammit you do what I tell you this time. Why the hell did you do that?"

"You?" she fought again. "Hurt?"

"No, I'm not." Another man joined Richard in her periphery and he added something to her chest. The pressure sucked at her, blackness dragging her down. "Dammit, Kate, why did you do it?"

"Had to protect..." And the world narrowed to two sharp pinpricks. She couldn't breathe.

You're okay.

That was worth a bullet or two.

∼

RICHARD

Intermittent calls for doctors and nurses punctuated the silence in the private waiting room. He'd ridden to the hospital in the ambulance, and Armand's security followed. It didn't surprise him to find another half dozen in place at the hospital or that more filtered in as Armand arrived with Anna on his arm. They were dressed for a formal event, but his best friend ignored the bloodstains covering Richard's chest and arms for a hard hug.

"You're okay." The shaken words might have sounded like a weakness in a lesser man, but Richard recognized the relief in his best friend's voice and the fierceness in his grip. He gave the man a moment, then pulled back. Anna leaned in and gave him a hug, no words required.

"Kate?" she asked softly. As she pulled back, pink stained her white gloves. Some of the blood on him—Kate's blood remained wet.

"She's in surgery." He focused on the cream-colored wall behind her. The scene—the gun firing, Kate being hit by bullets meant for him—replayed in constant, shuttering clarity in his mind. Not once, but twice in as many months the woman he loved took a bullet for him.

Loved.

Love. The woman I love.

He loved her and some part of him recognized it, but the rest of his mind hadn't been ready to embrace the concept. She slotted so neatly into his life, the perfect complement from work to home and back again. The smoothness of the transition had been so damn seamless—even in her anger over his "absences" and his ducking of security, she belonged.

Why the hell didn't I see it before?

"They need someone to make some decisions, I've been trying to reach her mother, but I haven't gotten an answer yet." He needed to think and he couldn't past the roaring. *You? Hurt?* The bubble of blood on her lips, the frantic worry kindling in her voice as the light faded in her eyes. *Had to protect...*

She'd done it on purpose. No matter how many times he tried to analyze what happened, he'd seen her step right into the path of that bullet. A soldier, she'd been in the army—she didn't stumble or make a mistake. The decision came in a split-second. She'd looked from the gun to him and then she was just there.

Scrubbing his face with his palms, he swallowed the scream working to break loose out of his throat. *No, she is not going to die...*

"Richard, what can we do?" Anna's hand was on his arm, her face a concerned mask. Of course she was concerned, Kate had worked with her. They'd been friends. *Are friends, dammit. Are.*

"I don't have any ties to her that let me do it." He'd been telling them about Kate. Telling them what he needed. "Can you call her mother? Her father? She has a brother in Germany." *Beany baby. I couldn't say Ben when I was little and it came out Bean. They called him String Bean, but one day I called him Beany Baby and it stuck.* "His name is Benjamin. He's in the army. Maybe call them? I can call them." He touched his pockets, looking for his phone.

"I'll do it, Richard. I'll do it." Anna squeezed his arm and turned away. She paused at Armand's side and hissed. "Tell him. He needs to know. You *tell* him."

He didn't have his phone. No, he'd dropped it at the house when the man showed up at the door. He'd put a gun to Kate's head and Richard had dropped everything. *You want to shoot me? Fine. Shoot me.*

Fierce. His Kate had been so fierce. He hadn't seen a glimmer of fear in her eyes until that moment.

Just like when they'd been shot at on the street, she'd focused all of her concern on him.

"Richard," Armand's hand was on his shoulder. "Come on, sit down."

"I don't want to sit. They need someone who can make decisions for Kate." He was repeating himself.

"I know. Peterson is taking care of it. Come sit down." Armand didn't take no for an answer—he walked Richard over to the seat. No one came into the room. Anna had apparently taken her phone outside.

"Is Anna okay? She shouldn't be alone."

"She has her detail with her, she'll be fine. Richard, I need you to focus."

Of course she did. Armand protected the woman in his life. She didn't take bullets for him, he wouldn't allow it. He didn't allow anyone close to him to get hurt, not if he could...

"*Miranda quit. Just up and quit. I'm supposed to be back in the office tomorrow and she called me on the way here to tell me she came into an inheritance and she's off to do the world cruise and traveling she's always wanted to do. What the hell am I supposed to do now?*" He was sick to death of being stuck in his house and he'd finally gotten the all clear from the doctor. He'd agreed to wait until Monday only because he wanted Armand's babysitters off of him.

"*Anna's assistant might be a good fit, you met her once—Kate Braddock?*" Armand grinned. "*Anna doesn't need her as much with the scholarship off the ground, I can talk to her see if she'd be interested.*"

"*If she is, it would save my life.*"

He turned slowly and stared at his best friend. A man he'd known since college—the prince who wanted to be like everyone else, but he'd never been ordinary. Powerful and intelligent, he'd grown only more so after his father died and he'd inherited the role of grand duke and head of his family.

Someone has to make decisions for Kate.

I know. Peterson is taking care of it.

Peterson. The royal family's security chief and Armand's left-hand man in the United States. Armand was ruthless, cunning, and possessed enough deviousness to get his way when he wanted it. There wasn't anything he wouldn't do to protect the people he loved.

Paying off an assistant and installing a bodyguard right under Richard's nose so that he'd be protected whether he liked it or not? Not even a stretch.

"You son of a bitch."

"Yes." Armand nodded once. "I did what I had to do, to keep you safe. You didn't want a security detail, wouldn't hear of it until after Kate got hurt. She was part of Anna's—"

Richard bounded to his feet and paced away. Of course Kate was a bodyguard. She had the requisite skillset. She'd been military and she joked about how she kicked that Kuwaiti prince's ass. She was always watching, observing, and tracking the movements of people around them. When she walked into a room, she assessed it. She anticipated his needs and she made changes. They'd been subtle at first, but little by little she'd brought him to heel.

He'd joked about her managing him, but that's *exactly* what she'd done. Managed him and the situation because Armand hired her to be his bodyguard. And his "sneaking" out and shedding his security—it had infuriated her.

"Richard." An olive branch wrapped in an order tied to an obligation.

"Go to hell." He did not want to hear the excuses or his bullshit about having to protect the people around him. As if his title gave him the right to make decisions about people, to put Kate into harm's way.

"I've been there. I was there just a few months ago when they pulled you out of your car. They had to peel back the metal, Richard. I saw the car afterward. It's a miracle you survived. I sat in this hospital and I prayed for hours that you would come through that surgery and once you were out, it was still touch and go. You lost a spleen and a kidney. Yes, I'm a bastard. I hired that woman and I told her that her only job was to keep you alive. I didn't care how she did it, or what she had to do—"

Richard spun and slammed his fist right into Armand's big, damn mouth. The prince staggered. Two of the security men started forward, but Armand waved them back.

"You told the woman I love that her only job was to take a bullet for me because *you* decided that. You didn't have the right, *Your Highness*."

"I had *every* right." Armand's eyes blazed and he got right in Richard's face. "You are my *best* friend, my *brother*. You can be pissed at me all you like, but I'd do it again in a heartbeat. You're *alive* because of that woman in there and I pray she survives so I can kiss her hand and thank her for saving you."

"Saving me? You *damned* me, Armand. I fell in love with a lie! A lie you hired and paid because you have to be in control of everything. I'm your *best friend*? No—I'm your ex-friend and in the morning, I won't be your attorney anymore." He pivoted to walk away.

Armand grabbed his arm. "You don't want to do this right now. You're upset and you're not thinking clearly."

That was a joke and it was on him. Richard laughed. "You know, I think I'm seeing clearly for the first time in a long time. Everybody lies to get what they want. My father, you—Kate. Everybody lies. I am sick to death of the lies. Now get your hand off me or you will need your security put your face back together." He cut a cold look at him. Needed the cold. Needed to shut it all out. "Because I'm done."

Armand released him and Richard strode away. He was at the door when Armand called, "Stay long enough to see her."

"Why?" He turned and spread his arms wide. "Her job is done. Be sure you give her a bonus. That's three bullets she took for our friendship, Your Highness. This..." He swept his hand over himself. "This is her blood. My consolation prize for being the idiot who fell in love with her. Congratulations. I'm alive."

Turning around he stared into Anna's tear-filled eyes. "Richard, don't do this. Don't walk away."

"Your prince is that way. Good luck. You're going to need it." He ignored the flash of hurt in her eyes and cut around her. He had to get the hell out of that hospital and away from them and the lies.

I love her. I'm a fucking idiot. I'm in love with a lie.

The truth should have set him free, but all that knowledge brought was more pain.

CHAPTER 13
RICHARD

He made it as far as the curb of the emergency room exit when he realized he didn't have his car. Glancing around the darkened parking lot, he swore and started for the street. He'd find a taxi.

"Mr. Prentiss?" Peterson's voice cut through the darkness. "If you'll give us one minute, we'll have a car here for you."

Richard stopped. He was covered in blood. If he made it to the curb, he'd probably end up with a police ride home. "Fine."

The men who'd followed him out fanned around him in a semi-circle. Peterson came to stand next to him on the curb. "The man who fired the weapon was named Leonard Braun. His father invested heavily in your father's confidence scheme and the family lost everything. They never recovered. Leonard, however, had other issues including a diagnosed clinical depression. He went off his meds over a year ago—

right around the time the story broke about the Princess Alyxandretta."

He tried not to listen, but the man kept right on speaking.

"The police have begun a thorough search of his apartment—a source informed me he had several news clippings regarding you, specifically in your capacity as attorney for the family, as well as other notable cases. They also found surveillance footage and a damaged vehicle in his garage. We're assuming paint on it will match the color of your car." Peterson paused when an SUV paralleled the curb right in front of him.

Jerking the handle, Richard slid in, but Peterson blocked him from closing the door.

"You are angry and feeling manipulated by the situation. That is your right." The man's tone might have been neutral, but his hard assessing gaze was not. "However, while Braun seems to have been working alone, there are two simple facts you need to be made aware of."

The man apparently would not let him go until he'd said his piece. Richard stared at him and waited, because he sure as hell wasn't explaining himself to another of the prince's employees. "And they are?"

"Your life was under threat, and it is not unlikely that you won't face similar threats in the future with your increased profile." Peterson tapped the car door. "Ms Braddock quit more than a month ago. She called me and explained that her level of personal involved compromised her ability to protect you. She resigned as your personal protection and requested permission to tell you the truth."

"Is that it?" *A month ago.* The weekend after she'd been shot the first time. She'd been so opposed to personal involvement and then—

And then she'd come downstairs and he'd seen the choice shining in her eyes.

"Yes, Mr. Prentiss." Cool disapproval hummed in the words. "Unless you want to know a status on Ms Braddock?"

He intended to say no, but instead said, "Is she going to be all right?"

"The first bullet punctured her lung. They had to reinflate it. The second nicked her bowel wall, but they assure me it is repairable. The surgery is complicated and could be a few hours. If at any time you want a prognosis, ask one of my men. They'll call me." Peterson backed up a step.

"Take care of her." The adrenaline and anger had fled. He was exhausted. Closing the door at the man's nod, he leaned back in the seat.

"Your house, Mr. Prentiss?" The driver asked in a tone as carefully neutral as the security chief's.

His house. The bed he shared with Kate. The life he'd begun to construct around her with every intention of keeping her in it.

"No. The Beverly Wilshire. See if someone at the house can pack up some clothes for me and send them over. They should probably pack Kate's things as well."

"We'll take care of it, sir. Do you want Ms Braddock's things delivered to the hotel?"

"No. Peterson will know what to do with them." Richard closed his eyes. He didn't open them again until he was at the hotel. One of the men offered to book the room for him and another offered him a clean shirt. He stripped out of the bloodied clothes and passed them over.

Once in his room, he didn't sleep. He wanted to, but he couldn't. He replayed every conversation, every act, and every single moment he'd shared with her.

She resigned as your personal protection. Her level of personal involvement compromised her ability to protect you.

His mind wouldn't shut up. Showering, he washed until the last of her blood was off him and, when sleep remained elusive, he cracked open the wet bar.

~

THREE DAYS LATER...

"Wake up." Water splashed his face. The cold burned away the fog of sleep, but did nothing for the brutal hangover savaging his skull.

"Get out, Armand." Richard buried his face in the pillow. His mouth tasted like ass and his head didn't feel much better.

"You know, Richard, you've been a lot of things over the years, but you've never been a coward. Now get your stinking ass out of the bed and go take a shower. I'll order up some break-fast." Armand sounded disgusted. "And a maid."

Glancing blearily around the room, Richard shrugged. "I didn't let them in."

"Clearly."

"I don't want you here." He didn't want to be awake. It had taken a hell of a lot of alcohol to send him into oblivion. Why the hell couldn't Armand leave him there?

"That much is obvious and I gave you three days. Now get up and get in the shower."

"Or what?" Richard rolled over to glare at him. "You'll bring in a bodyguard to strong arm me in there?"

"No, I'll bloody well do it myself. Stop being an idiot." Armand picked up an empty bottle off the nightstand. "You drank an entire bottle of cabernet without a glass?"

"I ran out of whiskey." And the wine made him think of Kate and then he hadn't been able to stop thinking about her. Stumbling out of the bed, he kicked another bottle away from him. "When I get out of the shower, I want you to be gone."

"Well, I hope you're prepared for disappoint-ment." Of course, Armand would do whatever the hell he wanted.

Ignoring him, Richard went into the bath-room. He turned on the shower and managed to make it to the toilet before throwing up most of the liquor cabinet. Thirty minutes under the pounding pulse of the water and a cursory brushing of his teeth helped, but the hangover was preferable to the other ache—the uglier one inside—so he held on to it.

His room had been freshened—the debris cleared away and a table with food set up in the center. Armand stood at the windows, gazing at the city below. "There's coffee on the table and I kept the food order bland in case you needed to vomit again."

The coffee was an attractive enough offer, so he poured himself a cup. His prescription medicine sat in the center of the table and he stared at it. He hadn't asked for it from the house and the suits and clothes they'd sent over had only the most basic of toiletries.

"She asked me to make sure you had it, since you have a habit of forgetting them." Armand took the carafe and poured himself a cup. "Sit down."

"No." Richard shook his head. "You don't walk into my room and just start ordering me around—"

"Enough," Armand snapped. "Sit down before you fall down. I am not here as a prince, but as your friend. I let you pour yourself into a bottle for three days. You've never been your father, Richard, and this is a terrible time to start emulating him."

Shock turned him rigid and he sank down in the chair.

"Yes." His oldest friend nodded. "I know all about your father. I've always known. I know he is currently suffering from liver failure and has been trying to make amends for the first time in his sorry existence."

"You never said anything." Richard stared down at the cup of coffee, shame and embarrassment playing cold accompaniment in his soul.

"I assumed if you wanted to talk about him, you'd bring it up. You didn't, I left it alone. You built your own life." Armand leaned forward and clasped his hands together, and their gazes locked. "You carry an enormous burden of guilt for being happy after what your father did. You work twice as hard as any man should need to or have to. But the one thing about you I have never doubted was your honor. I thought—for a while—that you needed wealth to prove your success where your father failed. But it was never about the money. You and your pro bono cases, and your causes, and your charities. You're always trying to make up for what he did."

"It doesn't really matter now, does it?" Of course Armand knew. In hindsight, Richard had allowed himself to be blinded to the reality of being a prince's friend. "They did a background check when we became roommates."

"Yes."

"So you've known since we met."

"Yes."

"But you told me who you were." The weird, twisted sense of honor and brotherhood between them had been borne during that confidence sharing. A friendship that had sustained them both through some very dark times in Armand's life and in Richard's effort to build his own.

A single nod. "I hoped you would one day have enough trust to tell me, but when you didn't, I respected your need for privacy."

"Easy enough to do when you already had the answers." He drained the coffee and poured himself another. The dull throb in his head couldn't keep the memories away now. "How is she?"

"Recovering," Armand answered immediately. "Her mother is here and her brother is flying in from Germany. She'll be in the hospital for some time, and she'll need several months to heal, but she'll be fine."

Relief made him weak and he bowed his head. He'd half-expected to hear she'd died—he'd run as hard from that idea as he had her lie. He wanted to know more—craved it—but he didn't dare ask. They needed a clean break. "You're compensating her for lost time, right? I mean she kind of lost two jobs in the same day."

"She will be taken care of Richard. When have I ever not taken care of those people who are important to me?"

"Oh please." Anger surfaced and he bobbed on it like a life raft, it was easier to cling to the fury than to the pain. "She's someone who works for you."

"No, she's someone my brother loves. Which makes her my sister. I'll treat her accordingly, even if my brother is behaving like a jackass." Armand stood and dropped a passport on the table. "Go to Europe. Sebastian is in Florence. He's expecting you. Spend some time on his yacht, rest, recover and then come back here and get to work."

"You can't just send me out of the country. I don't work for you and I have cases." His interest in the fight waned. Couldn't Armand just leave him alone?

"No, I asked Daniel for some assistance and his attorney—Grange? He's taken over the cases at Christine's Center. All of your papers were filed and taken care of."

Guilt stabbed Richard. In his need to get blind, roaring drunk, he'd let a lot of things slide.

"As for the foundation, well, your associates will have a true test of their mettle. Fortunately, everything is settled with the consortium deals. You don't have to be there. Peterson's men will get you to the airport. My jet is waiting for you. Take a month, figure out what you want to do, and come back."

"And if I don't? Go, that is?"

"Well, then you'll find me here every day and I won't leave." His tone stiffened, and grew more formal. Oh, Armand was angry after all. "Anna is most cross with me about this entire situation. She blames me too. Perhaps you are both right, but I don't care. I am hardly going to let you kill yourself, nor will I stand idly by while someone else tries to do it. You need time and I can respect that—"

"But only on your terms." Richard dared him to disagree.

"In the world I live in? Yes. On my terms. But this isn't just about you, Richard. Kate nearly died to make sure you stayed alive. She asked about you the moment she woke up. She called your name and she wanted to know that you were alive. She didn't care about anything else."

A fresh lance of guilt splintered his heart.

"We told her we'd moved you to keep you safe. She'll buy that for a little while, she's on a lot of drugs. So man up, grow some balls, and figure out whether you really love her and can be the man for her. Be my friend again. We'll wait." He tapped the passport. "If you're still here in the morning, expect a roommate."

Armand made it to the door before Richard reached over to pick up the passport. "You're getting married in a month."

"I know. I really hope my best man is there." The door closed behind him and Richard stared at the blue cover. *What the hell did he want?*

Kate's face flashed before his eyes and he sighed. Dropping the passport on the table, he scrubbed his hands against his face. Maybe Armand was right, he couldn't think here. He hadn't been thinking—he'd been drowning and the prince threw him a life line.

No, not the prince. My friend. My brother.

Picking up the prescription bottle, he stared at it. Dammit. That woman. From a hospital bed, she was trying to manage him. Walking to the door, he pulled it open and the security guard gave him a questioning look. "Yes, Mr. Prentiss?"

"I want to go to the hospital."

❧

KATE

"A prince! You have princes coming to visit you in the hospital. And these flowers? Have you ever seen so many? I can't get over it, Katie. You told me you were working in security. I thought you meant rent-a-cop, instead you're all Jane Bond."

If her mother didn't stop talking soon, Kate thought she might find another gun and finish the job Leonard Braun had started. Shirley Braddock meant well, but she babbled when she was nervous and the constant stream of visitors including a prince, a princess, and the future princess had left her more than a tad disconcerted.

"Mom, its personal security and I don't know if I'll be doing it much longer." Not after screwing her last job up so epically.

"Hmm, I've heard that one before, dear." Her mother stroked her hair back. "I should go down to the gift shop and see if they have more of that freeze dried shampoo."

"Waterless shampoo? Sure, that'd be great." Anything to get a break from the chatter.

"Do you want anything else? A magazine? Crossword puzzle book? Book? I know, I'll just pick you up one of everything." She rose and kissed Kate's forehead. "Be a dear and don't pick on the nurses when they come in to check your vitals."

"Promise, I'll be good." *Gooooo.* But she swallowed back the snarl. Her mother hadn't stopped talking since she'd arrived and she'd been a nervous wreck.

Closing her eyes the moment the door closed, Kate sighed.

They'd told her Richard was fine, but she hadn't heard from or seen him. Yes, it made sense they'd lock him down for a few days to make sure that Braun acted alone. But she didn't get the feeling from the man that he was part of any larger conspiracy. It didn't matter that they'd loaded her up on painkillers, or that it was her lung that had been compromised and not her heart.

Because her heart hurt.

Opening her eyes, she stared up at the ceiling and then reached for the leads connecting her to the machines. If they had Richard on lockdown then she just needed to go to him. It was over—and she could tell him the truth dammit. Peterson said Braun was behind the accident and the first shooting.

Her job was done.

~

SHE MADE it to Richard's house, but he wasn't there. The guard at the gate recognized her, and without complaint, he'd helped her into the house. She'd been grateful—it had taken every scrap of energy she had to stay upright on the drive. Without a doubt, the guard would report in to Peterson and whomever, but it didn't matter.

Richard mattered.

Exhausted, she sank down onto the sofa and leaned her head back. Maybe leaving the hospital early hadn't been the best idea—though it proved surprisingly easy. What little energy she'd mustered evaporated before she slipped into a taxi. Bless the driver, he didn't bat an eyelash at her odd clothing.

Who knew, maybe pajama bottoms and a hospital gown would be all the rage in the next season.

The door opened and Kate could barely keep back a groan. "I asked for a few minutes," she told the guard, not willing to move yet. "I can go back to the hospital later."

"Kate." At the sound of his voice, her eyes jerked open.

"Richard." He was there. He looked like hell—his eyes were bloodshot, his hair disheveled, and his shirt wasn't tucked in—and she'd never seen a more beautiful sight. "You *are* okay." Relief swamped her.

"Yes." His presence seemed to fill the room, but there was a distance in his eyes and a hard tilt to his mouth. "You weren't at the hospital."

"Neither were you." But her attempt at levity fell flat and her relief dissolved into a pool of unease. "You know."

"Peterson had to authorize your medical care," he murmured. "I figured it out and Armand confirmed."

Her heart squeezed at the distrust in his dark eyes. "I'm sorry." She had no excuse to offer, no pretty words to make it better. They'd given her a

257

job to do and she'd lied to him to make it happen. "I lied to you."

"Yes, you did." A muscle in his jaw flexed. "Then you saved my life—twice."

How did she answer that? "I screwed up at the center. I shouldn't have let you distract me when I opened that door. I shouldn't have opened it without clearing the porch first. Basic rules and I—I was thinking about getting naked." Bitter was the taste of her failure.

"But you'd quit." He moved forward, his steps slow and his gaze intent. "That's what Peterson said."

The churning in her stomach increased. "I did. I still knew better, especially after you sent the security detail away."

"You were upset on the driveway." He said it as if that made sense to him now, and perhaps it did.

"An unsecure location? Strangers? Poor lighting? Yeah, I was upset. But instead of saying it, I had to keep playing my part." Tears burned in her eyes. Stupidity was crime in her book. "I'd never have forgiven myself if you'd been hurt."

"What part were you playing, Kate?" Danger lurked in that question, but he had every right to ask it.

"Girlfriend. Lover. But it wasn't a role, it was what I'd become." Her chest hurt with every breath, but she tried to take a deeper one. She needed to get the words out and refused to shy away from the choice she'd made. "It's why I had to quit. I hated lying to you."

"But you kept lying." The accusation stung.

She could argue that she'd made the decision before she really knew him—that it somehow mitigated it. "I had orders, and a contract and...all of that aside, I didn't want you to hate me."

"Ripping the Band-Aid off?" Her Richard appeared in the shadows of the cool man assessing her.

"Without mercy. I *liked* you. I really *liked* you. I never lied about my feelings. But it was so damn complicated. You were supposed to be a protectee, one I had to be undercover to protect because you didn't want visible security." She blew out a breath and tried to stand, because she hated feeling so weak in this discussion. But she'd barely made the attempt before Richard was across the room and stopping her with a hand on her arm.

"What are you doing?" There was nothing distant or cool in his growl.

"Trying to stand... To walk to you." Though his presence made her action a moot point.

"No, you stay there. Scared the hell out of me when I found out you'd slipped out of the hospital. At least until the man on the gate called Peterson and me to let us know you were here." He squeezed her arm gently, his fingers a light brush against her skin, but he pulled away before she could capture the contact then sat down on the coffee table in front of her. Blinking furiously, she catalogued his appearance. He really did look like hell.

"You didn't want visible security. They

briefed me on your aversion to it and the fact that you slipped a detail before. The job as your assistant was perfect. I'd be with you for a huge portion of the day, I could assess your internal security in the office, coax the building into increasing it, and provide the rest of the detail with the data on your schedule so they could maintain surveillance at a distance. It—it created an illusion that would make you comfortable and safe at the same time."

"Yeah, it's the illusion part I'm having a problem with." The stilted words were like shards of glass being driven into her chest.

"The job—as your assistant, that was an illusion that I enjoyed. I did do the work. You and me? That was..." How could she describe it? God, she'd wanted to be the one to tell him. Finding out the way he did and then... "You weren't under lockdown, were you?"

His lashes dipped once and his gaze slid away from hers. "No. I was drunk."

"Ripping the Band-Aid off?" She threw his words back at him.

"No, drowning the Band-Aid. I was angry and terrified. You bled you so damn much and I wanted to strangle you for trying to save me."

"Well, *you* told him to shoot you." Her anger surfaced. "You never tell a nutjob to shoot you, they just might do it."

"I didn't want him to shoot *you*." The words gritted out between his teeth were a fierce snarl and the distance in his eyes vanished to be replaced by fury. "He had a gun to your head, Kate.

He had a gun to your head and my heart stopped. All I could think about was making sure you got out of it alive."

She knew damn well where the gun had been pointed. "Without you it wouldn't have mattered," she whispered.

"Why?" He leaned toward her, their faces inches apart. "Why was it so damn important to do your job when you'd quit? Or was that an illusion too?"

"No, you jackass, I quit because I was falling for you and I couldn't be rational or reasonable about your security. I had to save you because I love you." She hit him, but the blow didn't move him. Not when she barely had any force behind it. "I love you."

He stilled, his gaze searching hers. "I want to believe you."

"Believe me or not, a man can be convinced of anything only if he wants to be convinced." She closed her eyes, but it was too late, a tear slipped out. "The scariest moment in my life happened when I saw him swing that gun at you. I knew I had seconds to act. Even though I hit the panic button, they would never get there in time."

"So you stepped into the bullet."

"I'd do it again." His face wavered through her tears. "I'd do it in a heartbeat. I don't want to be in a world that doesn't have you in it. I wasn't lying when I said I'd never met anyone like you before. You—blow my mind. You're so damn smart and so incredibly dedicated and you make me crazy. I loved every moment we spent together and I love *you*, Richard Prentiss. Call me a fool, call me a liar, call me anything you want. But I love you."

He cupped her face and brushed away one of her tears with his thumb. The utter gentleness in the action took her breath away. "I let you in, deeper than I have ever let anyone."

"I know." Her heart sank. Trust was a huge issue for him and she'd violated it. She'd violated it before she'd ever loved him. "If I could go back..."

"You'd change it?" He continued to stroke her cheek with his thumb, the hard line of his mouth softening. "But if you changed it, I wouldn't have met you."

"I could have told you the truth, that day in your office." It was bravado. Peterson would never have given her the job if she couldn't maintain the confidentiality.

"I would have thrown you out on your sweet ass." His lips curved in a hint of a smile.

A flash of humor raced through her. "You could have tried. You forget, I'm damn tough."

"No, I haven't forgotten at all." His tone gentled. "You keep proving your strength to me over and over. If you'd told me the truth then, I wouldn't have gotten to know this wildly capable woman with her ability to manage me so finely tuned she does it while recuperating from multiple gunshot wounds."

"His Highness brought you your prescriptions." Another weight lifted off her shoulders. He was so bad about remembering them.

"Okay, before we go any further— Again, His Highness is named Armand. He called you a sister today, so you can call him by his name to his face. Or jackass, or pain in the ass, or son of a bitch—I highly recommend all of those. But no more formality with him."

Surprise flickered through her at his fierceness. "Richard..."

"No, I'm not done. You had your turn, now it's mine. You can't bodyguard anyone anymore. No more stepping into bullets, no more Wonder Woman. I know you can and I think you're brilliant because you do it so fearlessly, but my heart can't take it. So I need you to tell me you've retired from that."

Laughing through a fresh wave of tears, she winced. "Okay, don't make me laugh, that hurts."

"Yeah, you still haven't said you're retiring."

"I don't really think it's going to be a problem after I ditched Peterson at the hospital." The security chief had been on hand every day since she'd been admitted and she'd gone out of her way to avoid him in the hospital.

Concern mixed with curiosity filled his tired eyes. "How did you get out of there?"

"You don't seriously think you're the only one who knows how to avoid a security team, do you?" Taking a shallow breath, she shifted on the sofa and sat forward. Not having the pressure on her back or her chest helped. Richard watched her like a hawk, but when he would have spoken, she pressed two fingers to his lips. "I'm not a big fan of the undercover bodyguard job and to be honest, I took this work because I have a pretty specific skillset. I like protecting people."

Brushing her fingers with a kiss, he caught her hand in his. "I can learn to adapt, just not a fan of you being shot."

"Well that makes two of us and it occurred to me the other night...before I got shot, that what you do for those women? At the shelter? You're amazing. That's why you have all those clothes upstairs."

A singular nod. "Sometimes they need a swift escape and can't take anything with them. Some need to be relocated to other states or be somewhere they're sure no one will find them. I can bring them here, they can come and go via the back and they *feel* safer and it helps them to make the decisions that are right for them."

He really was one of the white hats. "You do realize that if you'd told Peterson and your security team, we might have looked to the ex-husbands and abusers for a potential threat against you." Keeping it a secret may have protected his clients, but it had left him unguarded.

For a long moment, consternation arrested Richard's expression. She expected him to argue, but instead he sighed and gave a slow nod. "You're right. I didn't want guards because it threw me back to my childhood—to the FBI watching us and digging through my life. I *really* didn't think anyone was after *me*."

Because she adored him, she threaded her fingers with his. "That man wasn't really after you, so in that you were right. You're one of the good guys—the real deal. You take a risk with yourself and not for any reward but to help others. You're amazing man, Richard." He was too. He'd let himself bleed, take any hit for another, but for some reason he didn't think others should do it for him.

"It was about my father." With a sigh, he slid a hand up to cup her nape and leaned his forehead to hers. "I am so sorry that he was the reason you were shot."

"No, I was shot because I wanted to save your life, because yours means more to me than my own." She told him honestly. "Don't let the actions of a man made mad by grief, and mental illness, color any of this. Yeah, maybe your father screwed his family, but Leonard Braun's actions were his own."

"Except..." Of course he wanted to argue it.

"No," she shook her head and the gentle friction where their foreheads brushed offered comfort and connection. "No. *You* did nothing wrong, except keep some key details from your security team. *I* did nothing wrong except let myself get distracted from my training. At the end of the day, Braun chose to come at you with a weapon, to make you pay for those slights against him, real or imagined and he's in custody, you're safe and I'm—"

"Hurt."

"But I'll recover and I thought you said my scars were sexy." Her tease had the desired effect, the hard line of his mouth softened into a smile.

Then she sobered. "What about your father, though? What will you do?"

Richard shrugged. "To me—the big man I loved and admired died when I was a kid, and it disrupted my whole world. The man who took his place? The selfish jerk who trashed so many lives? That's not my father."

Her heart twisted for him, but she could understand the need to distance himself.

"But—I can't make decisions for Barb." At the mention of his sister, he frowned. "I'll call her. If she wants—if she wants anything to do with him, I'll be there. I'll help her." Without a second thought for how it might hurt him. God, the man needed a keeper, someone to protect him. "I can't ask you to quit," he said suddenly. "I want you to, but—"

She stopped him again with a kiss. "I was already thinking that a change might be necessary. Like I said earlier, I have a pretty specific skillset. Don't suppose you know anyone who could use someone like me?" Like the women at the shelter —she knew Richard helped some disappear and restart their lives. She could protect them.

"You can interview for the position of my assistant. I lost the last one due to some meddling by a certain jackass royal who's about to have his hourly rate climb exponentially."

"Really?" Kate cleared her throat. "That sounds very challenging."

"Quite." He nodded. "I'm not going to lie to you. The job won't be easy and will demand travel at least forty percent of the time. Where I go, you go. When I need a file, I need you to pull it up. You have to anticipate last minute changes and I may be calling or texting you at three in the morning to come in because we have to have a brief in front of a judge at eight."

"That won't be a problem. I'm used to a tough schedule and travel. Of course, I'll need to get out of the hospital first."

"True, you will need plenty of recovery time." Richard traced the outline of her mouth. "At least a month or more."

"I believe the recommendation from the physician would concur. I was remarkably lucky, but I should probably not rush it." Daring to hope, she pressed a kiss to his fingertips. "But I have to ask, do you think we can work well together? Do you have any particularly annoying habits that I might object to? Are you a vegetarian perhaps? Or someone who speaks with their mouth full of food? Do you eat while you dictate your notes? Do you prefer MP3s or in person dictation? What types of confidentiality contracts am I expected to sign? Will I receive any type of additional compensation for the level of disruption in my life? When you have romantic liaisons will you expect me to wait in the other room on the off chance of a three-a.m. emergency?"

"We work exquisitely well together, and the only annoying habits I have are that I have been called impossible on more than one occasion." Heat kindled in his eyes and the last of the shadows drifted away. He shifted, and pulled a prescription bottle out of his pocket. "The only time I talk when my mouth is full is when I'm devouring you."

Electricity tingled through her. "I do recall that habit...on more than one occasion."

He thumbed open the top and poured two pills out into her palm. It was *her* prescription. "And you know about how I dictate my notes and where—and when. But what about you?" Rising, he crossed the room to the kitchen and returned a scant moment later with a bottle of water. "Do you have a boyfriend or significant other that will object to my calls at three a.m.?"

After swallowing both and washing them down with a drink, she said. "There's only one man in my life that may object, and since he's the one offering me the job, he'll know exactly where I am at three a.m."

"Naked and in my bed," came the very firm order. But she didn't mind it, because that was exactly where she wanted to be.

"Richard? Do you think you can forgive me?"

"I already have." He pressed his lips to hers in a soft, very chaste kiss that still managed to curl her toes. "I love you, Kate. Everything else we can figure out—and Armand is sending us to the Mediterranean. I hope you like Florence and yachts and very expensive vacations."

Delight curled through her. "Oh?"

"Oh yes, you need to recover and I need you."

Her cell phone buzzed where she'd left it on the table and she grimaced at her mother's name appearing on the caller ID. "I don't suppose you could run interference with my mother?" In all likelihood, Shirley Braddock had turned the hospital upside down when she'd realized Kate left.

"Running interference is what I do best." Richard grinned and picked up her phone.

"No, it's not," she told him, but he'd already answered and he raised his eyebrows in silent inquiry. She mouthed the words "you love me."

"Hello, Mrs. Braddock, Kate's fine. She's at my house and I'll get her back to the hospital immediately," Richard said, his smile growing. "Yes, this is Richard Prentiss, the man who loves her."

EPILOGUE

RICHARD

Richard held his chin up while Kate adjusted his tie and then smoothed the dove gray, double-breasted vest. Satisfied, she dusted off his shoulders and took a step back. "You look very good." All of the men in the wedding party were in one-button morning suits and striped trouser sets. Fortunately, Anna had forgone the hats.

"No one is going to be looking at me." He cupped her chin and nudged her face up for a kiss. Kate's face shimmered with vitality. Their one-month in the Mediterranean had turned into nearly six weeks. He'd juggled his workload and kept up on his cases, but they'd sailed from one end to the other and frolicked—once Kate had healed enough to do so.

They'd only returned to the States a week before—just in time for Armand's slightly delayed wedding. "So, a ranch in Montana for summer escapes, at least three four-day weekends, and spring in Belgium for conferences, and at least a

271

week in Norway for the annual gathering with the Grand Duchess."

"Weekends off, Saturday *and* Sunday mandatory. Put more contract draft work on your associates. You can still review them all," Kate countered. "And do you really want a Montana ranch?"

The corner of his mouth curved. "You agreed to marry me."

"I have no recollection of that event, Mr. Prentiss." The smile in her eyes played havoc with his system.

Dipping his head down, he went to kiss her mouth again and she turned to give him her cheek. "Hmm. Let's see if I can remind you, our living room? I asked you to marry me."

"Actually, no you interviewed me for a job." A smile warmed her mouth. "Among the requirements were regularly being naked, for which I have no objections. However, the concept of marriage wasn't actually broached until we were on the yacht and since I was on painkillers at the time, it's questionable whether I had the mental capacity to enter into any kind of an agreement."

"I see. That would make the validity of upholding that argument difficult," he agreed and traced a finger down the column of her throat. "Difficult, but not impossible."

"It would take some legal maneuvering to make that agreement stick." He knew a challenge when he heard it.

"Ms Braddock, on the date in question, can

you describe your emotional state for me?" He lifted his brows.

"Well, I'd woken up from a major surgery a few days before and I'd taken an unsanctioned cab ride—"

"That was the house." He reminded her, aware of the door opening behind him. "I'm referring to our day on the St. Christos Islands near the Amalfi Coast."

"Hmm, Amalfi Coast?" Her expression turned thoughtful. "I'm afraid I don't quite recall that day. You gave me a full painkiller instead of a half because I'd had so much trouble sleeping. I spent most of that day drowsing in the sun on the forward deck while you cheated at cards."

"If you were drowsing, how do you know I was cheating?" He loved this woman. She never shied away from matching wits against him.

"Well, obviously cheating would have been mandatory. You were betting your future on a hand of cards against someone who didn't have the facilities to enter into such negotiations." Her tongue peeked at him from between her teeth.

"So essentially, the question of the agreement's veracity lies solely on your mental competency at that moment?"

Kate nodded once. "Yes."

"Is your judgment in anyway impaired this morning?" He dared her to deny it.

"To my knowledge, I am one hundred percent sober. I no longer require anything more than an aspirin for the lingering discomfort from my injuries. So, yes, I would say that my judgment is only impaired by the normal emotional reaction to attending a romantic wedding with a dashing man. Since the wedding hasn't actually started yet, we have a seventy percent certainty that I am not wavering based on some type of emotional overreaction." Her eyebrows wiggled up and down, pure merriment setting fire to the gold flecks in her eyes.

"Are you willing to certify that any agreements negotiated this morning would be made of your own choice, free from prescription coercion?" Better to clarify and make sure they covered all their bases.

"I would so certify, yes."

"In writing?" he pushed, but then that was in his nature. Her mouth curved into a smile.

"If necessary."

"Oh, it's necessary. But we'll get to that in a moment." Sliding his hand into his pocket, he pulled out a ring box. "Since you are of sound mind and exquisite body, let's state the terms of the contract for the record. Will you, Katherine Amelia Braddock, do me, Richard Michael Prentiss, the honor of becoming my wife?"

She moistened her lips and her breath hitched at the end of his request. "That's the offer?"

"You want the consideration?" He locked gazes with her, his soul in perfect lockstep with the fiercely strong woman in front of him. Her spirit and intelligence would never fail to amaze him.

"Absolutely. After all, any good contract must have those elements."

"They do, but you have to have acceptance in order to achieve consideration." He closed the distance between them, every molecule inside him leaning toward her.

"True. So the key here is for me to say yes?" She lifted her brows. "And what would the quid pro quo be?"

"You'll make me the happiest man on the planet and I'll spend the rest of my life trying to repay the favor—"

"Impossible," she murmured.

"I've heard that before." His voice lowered, his pulse beating only for her.

"No, I meant it would be impossible for you to spend the rest of your life achieving what you've already done. May I suggest a different quid pro quo?"

Delight filled him, but he kept his mind on the most important negotiation of his life. "Absolutely."

"You spend the rest of your life being you and you'll make me the happiest woman in the world."

"Only if you never stop being you," he added the caveat.

"Then, yes, Richard. I'll marry you." Her smile lit him up from the inside out.

"I want that in writing." He flipped the box open. "Witnessed and filed, in perpetuity, binding with no way to sever."

Tears swam in her eyes and she held up her left hand. "I can only give you my word right now, but as soon as we're done, I'll sign anything you want."

He slid his ring on her and something wrenched into the right place in his soul. She'd said yes and Kate was not the kind of woman to go back on her word. "Done." Bending his head, he caught her mouth in a sweet kiss that left his pulse racing and his blood hot.

A round of applause broke out around them and Richard glanced up to find Armand, his brothers and their security grinning like idiots. "You two are certifiable," George, the youngest of the three brothers, announced. "What kind of a wedding proposal requires legal negotiation?"

"The best kind," Kate declared and leaned into Richard's arms.

Laughter and a round of congratulations followed. Kate drifted over to speak to Sebastian. Richard glanced at his best friend, who did his best not to fidget despite his violent attention to the clock. "Nervous?"

"Incredibly." He sounded mystified by the idea. "Have you forgiven me yet?"

"Does it matter? You would still have done exactly what you did."

"Yes." Armand faced him. "It matters."

It did, but at least he wasn't sweating the last few moments before he married the woman he'd lost for nearly a decade. "Tempted to make you suffer a little longer, but yes. I forgive you. Don't do it again."

"I'm sorry, I thought you were acquainted

with me." But the last lines of tension around Armand's eyes eased and gratitude showed in them. Demanding, full of pride and definitely a man who liked to be in control, Armand could be nothing else. The strain between them had cost them both.

"True, but I think it's only fair to mention that if you do pull a stunt like this again, you understand I'll kick your ass."

"You don't scare me." He chuckled. "I have security."

"I have Kate." Richard grinned wider and glanced over at the woman who held the key to his heart. She met his gaze with a smile full of promise. "I win."

~

TO ENJOY MORE SCANDALOUS SECRETS, royal redemption, and a prince willing to break every rule to win back the woman he can't live without —grab Some Like It Secret, Book 4 of *Going Royal.*

AFTERWORD

It's always a pleasure to share an old favorite with new people. If you enjoyed this, keep an eye out for more old favorites to return after I they get re-edited and updated. Also, if you want to check out more of my stuff, I can't wait to see what you think!

xoxo
Heather

Website:
heatherlong.net
Reader group:
facebook.com/groups/heatherspack

About Heather Long

I *love* books. Not just a little bit, but a lot. Books were my best friends when I was growing up. Books didn't care if I was new to a town or to a class. They were always there, my trustiest of companions. Until they turned on me and said I had to write them.

I can tell you that my own personal happily ever after included writing books. I've always said that an HEA is a work in progress. It's true in my marriage, my friendships, and in my career. I am constantly nurturing my muse as we dive into new tales, new tropes, new characters and more.

After seventeen years in Texas, we relocated to the Pacific Northwest in search of seasons, new experiences, and new geography. I can't wait to discover what life (and my muse) have in store for me.

Maybe writing was always my destiny and romance my fate. After all, my grandmother wasn't a fan of picture books and used to read me her Harlequin Romance novels.

Follow Heather & Sign up for her newsletter:
www.heatherlong.net
TikTok